GiANT

GiANT

KATE SCOTT

Illustrated by Alexandra Gunn

Piccadilly
PRESS

First published in Great Britain in 2017 by
PICCADILLY PRESS
80–81 Wimpole St, London W1G 9RE
www.piccadillypress.co.uk

A CIP catalogue record for this book
is available from the British Library.

ISBN: 978-1-84812-564-3
also available as an ebook

1 3 5 7 9 10 8 6 4 2

Typeset in Bembo by
Palimpsest Book Production Ltd, Falkirk, Stirlingshire

Printed and bound in Great Britain by Clays Ltd, St Ives Plc

MIX

Piccadilly Press is an imprint of Bonnier Zaffre Ltd,
a Bonnier Publishing company
www.bonnierpublishing.com

For Sara Grant

See this? You probably think that the person the size of a shrub is standing in a forest, next to the trunks of some very large trees.

Those trees are my family. That shrub next to them? That's me.

It Didn't Start Well

Mum and Dad probably didn't mean to land me in trouble as soon as I was born. To be fair, since they were unusually tall, and Dad's brothers were unusually tall, and their parents were unusually tall, naming me Anzo must have seemed like an obvious thing to do. In case you don't know, in ancient German, *Anzo* means 'giant'. Which is a problem when it turns out that you're definitely *not* a giant. And an even bigger problem if you're unusually short. Maybe if I'd been named something normal, like Tom, Josh Gurney wouldn't have thought of lifting me up and hanging me on a coat peg, saying, '*Now* you're a giant!'

But I'd never know because I was stuck with being Anzo – and a shrub.

* * *

The day I thought my luck had changed didn't actually start well. At the end of first break, Miss Bentley came up behind me, gripped me by the shoulders and pushed me towards the Tadpoles classroom. 'Don't be late, little one,' Miss Bentley said, in her I'm-speaking-to-the-babies voice.

At All Stars Primary School our classes are split up by the stages of a frog's life cycle. So Reception and Year 1 are Tadpoles, Years 2, 3 and 4 are Froglets and Years 5 and 6 are Frogs.

I am in Year 6. I am not a Tadpole, I am a Frog.

When I turned round, Miss Bentley's hand flew up to her mouth. 'Oh, I'm sorry, Pea— I mean, Anzo,' she said. Then she did one of those giggle-coughs that grown-ups do when they're not supposed to laugh but can't help it. 'I keep thinking you belong in Tadpoles, don't I?'

'Yes,' I told her.

Miss Bentley knelt down and fixed me with her big brown eyes. 'I am so, so, sorry,' she said.

'That's OK,' I said.

In case you're wondering, I was lying.

It wasn't just Miss Bentley pushing me towards the Reception class. It was that she'd been about to use the Nickname. She'd been about to call me 'Peanut'.

There are lots of names for short people, and I've been called them all – Smurf, Shrimp, Squirt, Shorty McShortShorts . . . but the one I hate most is 'Peanut'. When you're so short that people regularly think you're five years younger than you actually are, and when people can lose track of you when you're standing next to a traffic bollard, you don't want to be reminded of it every second of the day. And 'Peanut' is the kind of name that doesn't let you forget.

In the afternoon we had a school trip to Lyme Regis. We live in a small town near the southwest coast. Any time the teachers want to take us somewhere educational, they take us to the beach. (Everyone at our school is really, really good at rock-pooling.)

We all filed onto the coach and then Mr Dooley got on, walked to the middle and did his head count.

'Where's Anzo?' Mr Dooley called out.

Everyone on the coach started to laugh.

'What is it?' Mr Dooley snapped. 'Is Anzo off sick?'

'He's definitely sick of being small, sir,' Josh Gurney shouted out.

In case you haven't guessed it by now, Josh is not a friend of mine.

I got up from my seat and walked up to Mr Dooley. 'I'm right here, Mr Dooley,' I said.

Mr Dooley looked down. 'Where've you *been*, Anzo? You know we need to leave for the trip punctually if we're to get back in time for the end of school.'

The thing about grown-ups is that they aren't interested in explanations. Mr Dooley didn't even wait for my answer. He was already pushing me towards a seat. That's another thing about being short – people push you around all the time. They seem to think if you're small, your legs must need a helping shove.

'What you want,' Elise said as we walked down the beach, 'is a megaphone. You could use it whenever Mr Dooley is trying to find you.'

Elise and I have known each other since we were three. We couldn't stand each other then (she used to hit me over the head with her panda and I'd pelt her with my rhinoceros) but we've become friendly since we discovered that we both like comics. Also, Elise is quite small for her age.

'What I *want* is to be a foot taller,' I told her.

'You will be,' Elise told me. She said that every time I complained about my height. I didn't know how she could be so certain. In the last two years, my *nails* have grown more than my legs have.

Then on the beach, when we were supposed to be searching for signs of marine life (in other words, rock-pooling), Josh decided it was time for another 'joke'.

'Hey, Anzo, he'd make a good donkey ride for you.' He came up to us, pointing at a large dog in the distance, then ran off laughing before I could make some cutting comeback. Not that I'd thought of one.

'Ignore him,' Liam said. Liam is in our class and we're pretty friendly, though we don't properly hang out after school or anything.

But it's hard to ignore someone who doesn't want to be ignored. Josh was now making hee-haw noises up ahead.

To make me feel better, on the coach on the way back I got out my mini-notepad and did a drawing of Josh as a donkey with big, stupid, floppy ears. Revenge with a pen. Josh will never see it so maybe it wasn't actually much of a revenge, but it did make me feel better. Sort of.

The worst bit of the day was when we got back to school. Everyone raced over to the noticeboard. I remembered that the school-play details were being announced. I followed with Elise, but didn't bother trying to get close. When you only come up to most people's armpits, you know to stand back and wait.

'Hey, Peanut, congratulations,' Josh said. Then he cracked up laughing. Josh has a laugh that sounds like someone sucking up the end of a milkshake with a straw.

Elise and I looked at each other. 'Uh-oh,' Elise said quietly.

Uh-oh was right. It was never a good sign when Josh laughed. Josh's sense of humour is based completely on other people's misery. The more miserable someone is, the more hilarious he finds it.

Just to remind you, Josh is not a friend of mine.

We went up to the noticeboard. Miss Bentley is in charge of doing our school plays. After the first couple of years she stopped holding auditions. She said it was because she didn't want anyone feeling traumatised by the audition process. But everyone knows it's because she'd struggle to get anyone to audition because of what's happened before.

The sign took up almost the whole board.

Snow White and the Seven Dwarfs
Adapted and scripted by
Miss Amelia Bentley

Cast:
Snow White: Geeta Naskar
Sleepy, Grumpy, Dopey, Sneezy, Happy,
Bashful and Doc: Anzo Oliver

I didn't read past that bit. I'm not sure anyone else did either. It wasn't just Josh who was laughing now. Everyone in Frogs, everyone in Froglets and even some of the Tadpoles were laughing – and some of the Tadpoles can't even *read*.

'You're *all* the dwarfs!' someone shrieked before collapsing giggling on the floor.

'Hey, Dopey!' shouted someone else. 'No, I mean Sneezy – I mean Bashful! I mean, Sleepy!'

'No, he's definitely Grumpy!' Josh yelled, and then fell about.

I backed away – right into Miss Bentley.

'Oh, Anzo, you've seen the good news!' She

crouched down, flicking her long hair out of her face (Miss Bentley is a real hair-flicking type). 'I've written the most brilliant lines for you – and I've designed seven different hats for you to wear.' She tapped her lips with her fingers. 'I may have to teach you a few different accents too.' She beamed at me. 'This production is going to be a triumph, I just know it!'

Miss Bentley didn't seem to hear everyone laughing. She didn't seem to hear the last remnants of my dignity rolling across the playground and down the school drain. She didn't seem to see my look of complete and utter horror, or Elise's glare.

Miss Bentley is not a teacher who notices much.

I wanted to say no. I wanted to tell Miss Bentley that there was absolutely no way I was going to be *one* dwarf, let alone seven, but everyone was looking at me, laughing, apart from a few, like Elise and Liam, who were just looking sorry for me. My skin got hotter and hotter. I opened my mouth but couldn't speak. Elise pulled at my arm. 'Come on, let's go,' she said, as the bell rang.

* * *

Later, Elise convinced me to go and talk to Miss Bentley on my own.

'You can't just accept it!' she told me. 'You have to tell her you don't want to do it.'

'It won't work,' I told her.

'That's negative thinking, not positive thinking. And negative thinking leads to negative outcomes. You have to lock up your negative thinking.'

Elise is great, but because she wants to be a therapist when she's older, she does sometimes sound like a textbook.

I had to agree with her though. I couldn't just accept it. So I went and found Miss Bentley at the end of school. But I guess I must have let my negative thinking loose by accident, because it didn't work.

Do you remember when you were little and trying to get a grown-up's attention? Maybe you wanted a drink, or a piece of cake, or to go to the park – but you couldn't get anyone to listen to you. You had to shout and shout and shout or tug their sleeve for *ages* before they even saw you. Because they were way up there, and you were way down here. That was what it was like being me. All the time. Except that it was worse, because when you're actually only four years old and you try and complain about how it's unfair, everyone says things like: 'Aw, I'm sorry, little man, we didn't mean to upset you.' Or, 'Hello sweetie, what was it you wanted?' When you're going to secondary school soon and you aren't cute, just short, that's not how it works; people just expect you to get on with it. That's how it was with Miss Bentley.

'Oh, Anzo,' she said, 'this is your last year at All Stars – don't you want to show everyone what you can do?'

'Not really,' I told her.

She wagged her finger at me. 'Now I know that deep down inside you is a performer just bursting to get out.'

'I don't think there is.'

'*Deep* down,' she repeated.

'I really don't think so.'

'So deep down it's almost like it's not there.'

I stared at her for a second and then tried a different tack. 'The thing is, I don't really like –'

I was going to say 'speaking in front of lots of people', but as I opened my mouth I pictured being onstage and I froze. The thought of all those people sitting in the audience, watching me as I opened my mouth to speak made me feel as if someone had set me on fire and superglued my feet to the floor. I'd tried not to imagine it before, but now that I had I couldn't get it out of my head.

'If you don't like the script when you see it, we can change it a bit,' Miss Bentley said. 'I don't mind a little bit of creative intervention. We can change a few words here and there.'

'But I don't want to say *any* words!' I probably sounded a bit desperate at that point. That was because I was.

'Oh, I see! You want to do *mime*!' Miss Bentley shook her hair back. 'Now that is a very interesting idea, Anzo. That might be even funnier.' She caught sight of my face. 'I mean, it could be a really rich source for dramatic possibilities.'

'No! I don't want to mime! I don't want to say anything! I don't want to be in it at all!'

Miss Bentley frowned and her ears turned a bit red. 'Pea— I mean, Anzo – I've done my best to accommodate your concerns, but you really can't expect me to take you out of the play altogether. I've built the whole thing around you! I can't just magic seven dwarfs out of thin air, can I?'

I tried to say something, but she'd spotted our head, Mrs Tyler, across the hall. She waved at her as she half turned back to me. 'Look, everyone gets a bit nervous when they first perform, but the whole thing will be very good for your confidence. And sometimes you just have to get on with things. After all, you'll have to do this kind of thing more and more as you grow up.'

I really didn't think being seven dwarfs was something I was ever going to be expected to do when I grew up, but before I could say so she smiled and tapped me on the head. 'But don't grow up *too* quickly – I need you to stay just the way you are for our wonderful show!'

I wasn't a massive fan of school at the best of times, but that day, I'd never been happier to leave.

Meet the Family

Before I tell you about the rest of that day, you'd better meet my family. Otherwise you might make the mistake of thinking that they're normal.

* * *

When you open the front door at your house, maybe you hear a television or a radio, someone making a cup of tea or preparing dinner, maybe the sound of dog barking hello. When *I* open *my* front door, I hear noise. Constant, ear-thrumming, eye-squinting, teeth-edge-setting noise. Drilling and singing and shouting and laughing and banging and then some more singing like a noise cherry on the top.

This is what Mum, Dad, Uncle Miles and Uncle Talbert are like: they think it's a waste of time to speak when you can shout, or to walk when you can run, or to smile when you can laugh. They believe in 'living life to the full' (Mum) and 'making the most of every moment' (Uncle Miles) and 'You could get run over by a bus tomorrow so follow your passions' (Uncle Talbert). Maybe you think that sounds fun. And it is – for them. But if you've spent your life trying to be heard by people who are busy living life to the full and making the most of every moment and following their passions in case they get run over by a bus, sometimes it's not fun, it's exhausting.

Uncle Miles and Uncle Talbert don't actually live with us (they share a flat down the road), but it feels like they do. About a year ago they decided to make Uncle Miles's dream of opening a restaurant come true. The problem was they couldn't afford to buy a restaurant, so they decided to turn our house into one. This is why the sound of drilling in our house is as regular as the boiling of the kettle (and my family drinks a LOT of tea). Uncle Miles is the cook, so he cooks all our meals (we eat a lot of experiments). Mum's in charge of all the alterations, which is why she's in a good mood pretty much every day. She's always loved DIY, and as long as she's drilling, nailing, fixing or thumping things, she's happy. Until the restaurant opens, Dad, Uncle Miles and Uncle Talbert are still running their bakery business (it's called 'A Piece of Cake'), with Uncle Miles doing the baking and Uncle Talbert and Dad making the deliveries and handling the marketing.

Dad and Uncle Talbert also really love to sing, so it all takes place to a musical soundtrack. They call themselves 'Volume 11'. That tells you all you need to know.

* * *

You'd think that after being missed on the coach (again), Josh's donkey 'joke', and finding out that I'd been cast as all seven dwarfs in the school play, the day would have been a complete fail. But it's like Uncle Miles says, sometimes there's honey in the sour cream. (With Uncle Miles's recipes, sometimes there really *is* honey in the sour cream.) When I came in that afternoon, sitting on the table in the hall was a letter addressed to me — and the return address on it made my heart thump. It was from the International Cartoon Strip Association. Two months before, I'd entered one of their competitions after seeing an ad at the back of my Spider-Man comic. Elise had made me send off my cartoon *Giant Versus Dr Slime*, even though I'd told her I didn't stand a chance.

I opened the envelope. The letter said that mine had been selected as one of the top-twenty entries. *Giant Versus Dr Slime* had been given an Honourable Mention in the Under-Eighteens category. I was so shocked I thought maybe I'd misread it. Maybe it said I *hadn't* got an Honourable Mention. But then why would they write to tell me what I hadn't got? I read the letter again. There it was — Anzo Oliver, *Giant Versus Dr Slime*, Honourable Mention. I was used to thinking of myself as below average (apart from my height, where I was well below — but you already know that), but the International Cartoon Strip Association was saying that out of over one thousand entries (*over* one thousand!) my cartoon was one of twenty to be picked out and sent a special certificate. I didn't even care that I hadn't got first, second or third place, because I knew what a long shot getting placed at all was. Even though I hadn't grown at all in the last eighteen months, I suddenly felt three inches taller. Maybe, just maybe, some things in my life were about to get a bit better.

I made my way to the kitchen. If I was lucky, Mum wouldn't be doing a DIY project for the restaurant today.

I wasn't lucky.

Mum had removed two cabinets from the kitchen wall and had her head inside one of them.

'Hi, Mum.'

My only answer was a clink as she yanked out a nail and threw it behind her onto the floor. Mum isn't big on tidying up, so you have to watch yourself in our house. It's not unheard of to reach for your toothbrush and find yourself picking up a wrench.

'HI, MUM.' I sometimes wondered if the reason my parents didn't seem to hear me was because their ears were so high up and my mouth was so low down. Maybe it was just an accident of geography.

'JUST A MINUTE,' Mum yelled from inside the cabinet. 'THIS NAIL IS PICKING A

FIGHT WITH ME. BUT DON'T WORRY, I'M GOING TO WIN.'

I stood with my certificate and waited. My family were usually busy doing something (usually something loud), so I'd got used to waiting around for them to be finished.

Eventually Mum extracted her head from the cupboard. 'Whoever fitted this unit did a real bodge job. It's a disgrace,' she told me. 'They used drywall screws instead of washer-head screws! Can you believe it?'

I had no idea what she was talking about, but I tried to look shocked.

She wiped her hands on her dungarees. Mum had a sort of uniform that she wore – dungarees or jeans, a scarf with some unusual pattern on it (like drills, or hammers, or nails, maybe even washer-head screws) and trainers in a bright colour. I could see that she was already twitching to get her head back into the cabinet. Once Mum had started a job, she didn't like to stop until she'd finished.

I held out the certificate. 'I got this today.'

Mum glanced down at it.

Guess what she said?

A. *Hey, this calls for a celebration! Let's go to Pizza Hut and order everything!* (No.)

B. *Wow! I'm so proud of you, Anzo.* (No.)

C. *You're the best comic-strip artist in the world!* OK, maybe a bit hopeful on that one. (And no.)

No, what Mum said was: 'It was probably very competitive, Anzo, don't worry – an Honourable Mention isn't bad at all . . .'

I knew that! I was about to tell her that it wasn't bad, it was actually very good (over a thousand entries!), when she went on as if she wanted to drop the subject as quickly as possible.

'Can you go and get the Phillips screwdriver? I think I left it upstairs.'

I guess she hadn't heard of the International Cartoon Strip Association (the greatest organisation known to cartoon-kind). And maybe she was just really worried about the kitchen cabinet. I thought about trying to explain, but then I remembered the other times I'd tried to talk to my family about my cartoons. They always said things like, 'That's nice – can you hand me that hammer?' (Mum) or, 'That reminds me, did I ever tell you about the time I drew a doodle on Mr Baldwin's bald head?' (Uncle Talbert) or, 'I don't know where you get your talent from – oh, yes, I do, it's me!' (Dad). So I went and got her the screwdriver and took my Honourable Mention letter up to my room.

I almost wished I hadn't told her so I could have kept the honey bit of the day to myself.

Dr Slime was up to his old tricks again . . .

He needed to be stopped . . .

. . . and fast.

It was time for Giant to teach Dr Slime a lesson.

It was time for Dr Slime to pick on someone his own size.

Or even someone a bit bigger . . .

Good Isn't
Good Enough

Dad and his brothers have a thing about 'being extraordinary'. To them, people shouldn't be trying to be good, they should be trying to be great. Maybe that's why they're always competing with each other. They compete over everything – and I mean *everything*. Once we were in a supermarket and Uncle Talbert said he was the fastest shopper so he should do it. Dad and Uncle Miles weren't having that of course. They made Mum divide up the shopping list between them. Then Mum and I had to watch their heads over the tops of the aisles as they rushed around from Vegetables to Freezer Goods at top speed with a shopping trolley each. It was like watching three street lamps on wheels. You could see the other shoppers were terrified – I saw four people abandon their trolleys and quietly leave.

Dad came first by about three seconds, but Uncle Talbert and Uncle Miles complained that he'd had the easiest items on the list and that they'd had to weigh the fruit and veg. They'd wanted a rematch, but the manager of the store overheard them (the whole shop probably heard them – it's hard not to when they're arguing) and threatened to ban them.

This kind of thing is not unusual. For Dad and my uncles, even laying the table for dinner can become a competitive sport.

Mum's not as competitive as Dad and my uncles, but she's a perfectionist and she's really big on doing things herself. That's why she loves the challenge of converting our house into a restaurant single-handedly. Or single-hammeredly.

What it all means is that impressing my family is pretty difficult, what with them all believing in being extraordinary and setting yourself big challenges and being independent. It's also difficult to get a word in.

* * *

The night I got the Honourable Mention letter, I came down to dinner feeling a bit nervous. I wondered if Mum would bring it up, or if maybe I should. Was this my chance to show them that I wasn't completely below average?

The noise coming from behind the kitchen door was threatening to blow its hinges off. I peeked in. Dad and Uncle Talbert were singing Elvis Presley's 'Blue Suede Shoes' at top volume while hanging homemade spaghetti to dry on the backs of chairs and some planks of wood Mum was going to turn into shelves. Uncle Miles was chopping vegetables with a large knife in a way that made me feel sorry for the vegetables. Mum had her head in another cabinet. In other words, it was a normal evening. I laid the table without Mum or Uncle Miles noticing and then waited in the dining room. Dad and Uncle Talbert came in first.

'Your harmony was a bit off in the chorus,' Dad told Uncle Talbert.

Uncle Talbert stopped in the middle of the room, grabbed Dad's arm and pulled a horrified face. 'Me? *My* harmony was off? My dear brother, have you completely lost your musical mind?'

Dad laughed. 'No, but you might have lost your musical ear.'

Uncle Talbert struck his hand to his chest. 'Oh, the injustice! The cruelty and the injustice! The cruelty and the injustice and—'

'The bolognese!' Uncle Miles announced, walking in with a large serving dish in his hands, followed by Mum, who still had a hammer in hers.

I sat down, but Dad and Uncle Talbert came closer to inspect the bolognese. Although they helped Uncle Miles in the kitchen (Uncle Miles called them his sous-chefs), Uncle Miles was the one who put all the meals together.

'What kind of bolognese is it?' Dad wrinkled his nose suspiciously.

Uncle Miles was what he called a 'creative' cook, and some of his creations were more successful than others.

Uncle Miles sniffed, offended. 'It's a perfectly bog-standard bolognese. Except for it being perfect of course.'

Dad gave a mock sigh of relief and sat down.

'And my genius addition of a smidgeon of smoked haddock,' Uncle Miles added, as he plunged in and started serving up.

'Oh, dear haddock in heaven!' Uncle Talbert groaned.

'You've got no imagination,' Uncle Miles told him.

'That's what you said about your horseradish cupcakes for the business, and look what happened there. Disaster!'

Mum laughed. 'Well, Miles only experiments on us for now, and I don't mind. As long as we've got a working menu by the time we open the restaurant.'

'In my opinion, we *have* a working menu,' Uncle Miles said. 'The working menu is my genius.'

'Yes, dear,' Dad said.

Uncle Miles sniffed huffily. 'You won't be laughing when I win my first Michelin star.'

'No, we'll be too busy being stunned,' Dad said under his breath, winking at me.

We started eating then (the bolognese was OK, though it had a bit of a funny aftertaste) and I waited to see if Mum was going to say anything about my Honourable Mention. Maybe she hadn't said much when I showed her because she was planning to announce it to everyone.

But Dad began a story about overhearing a customer in the local bookshop who'd been wanting 'that book about car racing by Bill Shakespeare'. Then that led to Uncle Talbert telling a story about acting in *Hamlet* at college when his codpiece had fallen off and how he'd decided to improvise and pretend it was a sausage. Then they all decided to see how many Shakespeare quotes they could remember (not many) and recited them in a Spanish accent (I can't remember how Spain got involved) and they were all falling about laughing. The only time I got included in the conversation was when Uncle Talbert asked me if we ever did Shakespeare for our school plays and I said, 'No.'

By the time we'd finished our bolognese I'd realised that Mum wasn't going to bring up my letter – and that I wasn't going to either. I couldn't face the possibility that Dad and my uncles would be even less impressed than Mum had been.

Maybe the Honourable Mention just wasn't good enough. I was going to have to try harder to get their attention. I was going to have to try and be extraordinary, like my family.

What Happiness Is

Upstairs, I settled down to draw the next bit of my new comic strip. Some people relax by listening to music, some play football or video games, I draw cartoons. I got into them when I was about six and Uncle Talbert gave me a book of Snoopy cartoons. It was called *Happiness Is . . . a Warm Puppy*. It was the three dots in the title — that little gap — which made me think it was more of a question. Was happiness a warm puppy? (I was six — I thought it was *definitely* a warm puppy. That, or chocolate ice cream.) I read the book over and over and started copying out some of the characters myself. Then after a while I started making up my own (my first one was *Doughnut Dog* about a dog who, no prizes for guessing, loved doughnuts). At first I showed my family, but though they smiled and nodded they never seemed to be that impressed, so after a while I stopped showing them anything and only ever talked about my cartoons to Elise. Elise understood that cartoons made me happy in a way that my family didn't seem to, even though they were always talking about 'following your passions'. Maybe it was because Elise had been studying the causes of happiness ever since she decided she was going to be a therapist. She figured that if she understood how happiness worked, she'd be more likely to help people find it.

I loved drawing cartoons more than I'd ever loved doing anything. I loved the way that you could make things happen from one frame to the next. Drawing pictures meant everything you drew was fixed, that it couldn't change. But comics kept everything moving, everything changing. And when I'd stopped growing a year or so ago, I'd realised what happiness was for me. It wasn't things staying the same, it was things changing. And that meant growing taller. Because if I was as tall as the rest of my family – or at least not so far below them – they might listen to me more, I might seem

more like one of them. Extraordinary, not
ordinary.

* * *

I'd just got to the second page of my latest
comic strip, *Giant Alone*, when the phone rang.
I picked up. (I was usually the only person in
the house who heard it.)

'Hello?'

'So I found this book in our house,' Elise said.
(She always launches in like this – it's not just
that she knows my voice from the first hello,
but she knows she doesn't have to say who it is
because she knows that I know that only she
would call me. The whole I know/she knows
thing is one of the reasons why we're friends.
Friends know a lot of stuff they don't have to say.)

'And?'

'I was looking through our books and I found
one that might be useful for you. You know,
with what you want.'

I sat up straighter. 'Yeah?'

'It's called *The Power of Positive Thinking*.'

'Oh.' I slumped down on the bed again.

'Give it a chance before you decide it's a load
of rubbish,' she said.

'I didn't say anything!'

'You said, "Oh," and I know what "Oh" means'.

(This is the not-so-good side of the I know/she knows thing.)

I heard Elise's bracelets jangling. Elise wears about fifty bracelets on each arm and they're always jangling. It's like being friends with a set of wind chimes.

'It says,' Elise went on firmly, 'that "Much can be accomplished by the dedicated chanting of your objective."'

'What does that mean?'

'It means that if you keep chanting, "I want to be tall," you will get taller.'

'Simple as that?'

'Simple as that.'

'I've been saying that for years,' I told her. Did Elise really think that talking to myself was going to get me what I wanted?

'Yeah, but not over and over,' Elise said. 'It says that for the chant to work you need to repeat it hundreds of times, really focusing on what you want.'

I didn't say anything. I was imagining myself chanting at school and everyone laughing at me. I mean, they laughed at me anyway, but it's not like I needed to give them an extra reason to do it.

'You don't have to do it *out loud*,' Elise said, reading my mind. 'And you don't have to do it all the time. Just do some first thing in the morning and last thing at night.'

'Hundreds of times.'

'As many as you can manage.' The bangles jangled again – she was getting excited now she realised I was considering it. 'And you're supposed to visualise your objective while you chant.'

'You mean imagine myself as tall.'

'Yeah.' The jangles went mad again – I guessed she was nodding. 'Look, why don't you give it a try? Even if it's not likely, isn't it worth a shot, just in case?'

When she put it like that, I had to agree.

* * *

So that's how I decided to give *The Power of Positive Thinking* a try. I mean, Elise was right – it couldn't make anything worse, and maybe, just maybe, it would make things better.

The first twenty times I chanted, 'I want to be tall,' I felt a bit silly. But around the thirtieth time, I started getting the hang of it. I tried emphasising different words.

I want to be tall, I *want* to be tall, I want *to* be tall, I want to *be* tall, I want to be *tall*.

It almost sounded like a musical rhythm. I rapped out the words with my fingers on my thighs.

Iwanttobetall I want to be tall I wanttobe tall . . .

I lost count in the end, but in the morning when I woke up the chant was there in my head.

I want to be tall, I want to be tall, I want to be tall . . .

I threw back my duvet and ran over to where I kept a measuring tape and a pencil (you would too if you were my height). I measured myself on the back of the door.

I hadn't grown a millimetre.

I want to be tall, I want to be tall, I want to be tall . . .

I guessed it had been stupid to think it was going to happen overnight.

Or at all.

Not All Families
Are the Same

Like I said earlier, Elise already knows exactly what she's going to be when she grows up. It's probably because Elise's mum and dad are both GPs who work at the same local practice. (One of her dad's favourite jokes is to say, 'We haven't got sick of seeing each other yet.') So it means Elise has grown up with the idea that making people feel better is a good idea (which, to be fair, it is). She doesn't want to be a doctor who deals with body stuff though, because although she's very interested in how the body works, the sight of blood makes her feel funny. Instead she's going to make people feel emotionally and mentally better. It's great that she cares about people and knows what she wants to do, but it does mean that she asks you how you're feeling a *lot*. And in the name of her happiness project, she's also always trying out different therapeutic techniques on people. Sometimes these work and sometimes they don't. Like when she recommended dance therapy to Celia Wanstead without realising that Celia has zero coordination. (Celia fell over trying out a jazz–contemporary jump and sprained her ankle.)

Anyway, Elise's family is completely and totally different to mine. For a start, while my house is full of planks of wood, hammers, nails and assorted tools (Mum), piles of forms to do with the restaurant (Dad and Uncle Talbert) and kitchen utensils and exotic spices (Uncle Miles), Elise's house is unbelievably tidy. Everything about Elise's house and Elise's family is organised. Everyone knows exactly what they're supposed to be doing and when. If Elise forgot her PE kit one day, her parents would remember to remind her. Not that she would forget in the first place. Elise is like her parents – she remembers *everything*. (She still remembers that when we were seven I once drew Doughnut Dog on her picture of a unicorn. I thought Doughnut Dog made it a better picture. She didn't. She didn't speak to me for a week.)

Elise's mum and dad organise their week entirely with Post-it notes. Their dinners are planned out on yellow Post-its, their shopping lists are on blue Post-its and weekly tasks on green. Even their holiday activities are Post-itted (pink).

And it isn't just Post-its. Every book in the house is shelved according to author name and subject. Clothes are folded in drawers and hung in wardrobes by colour and time of year. They have different cupboards for spring, summer, autumn and winter, and I once heard Elise's mum talking with Elise's dad about them needing an 'in-between season' cupboard, until Elise's dad pointed out that there was nowhere to put it.

While we ate whatever Uncle Miles felt like cooking that day, menus at Elise's house were drawn up on Sunday night. If you felt like macaroni cheese when it got to Thursday but the Post-it note said chicken stew, the Post-it won. In their house, no one argued with a Post-it note.

Her family also had loads of traditions. Traditions like watching a family film on a

Saturday night after having a Chinese takeaway, or taking a 500-piece puzzle away with them every time they went on holiday, or toasting marshmallows on the first night of the year it was cold enough to light a fire (August). Lots of ordinary, nice, comforting traditions.

My family didn't believe in traditions, they believed in being 'spontaneous'. Uncle Miles said if you had traditions it meant you gave up doing fun stuff at the last minute like going to the beach because the sun was shining or because you'd woken up in a particularly good mood. But when Elise told me about the first marshmallow toasting of the year and how her mum dropped hers in the ashes and ate it anyway because it would strengthen her immune system, I couldn't help thinking that traditions can be fun too. The last time we had a 'spontaneous fun day out', Dad, Mum and my uncles brought all the gear for an outside barbecue on the beach. It rained the whole time we were there and we had to cook the hamburgers in the boot of the car. The smoke made us all cough and the car stank of burgers for a week. That was the problem with my family. They were so busy being spontaneous that they never thought to check the weather forecast. Or anything else.

Of course Elise had the opposite opinion. She loved how 'free' our household was, and how there was always something going on. She said spending time in my house was like watching a rehearsal for a really good comedy show.

Maybe she was right but most of the time it felt as if I was the only one who hadn't been given a part.

* * *

Elise read me bits of *The Power of Positive Thinking* all the way to school. It wasn't just chanting you had to do. Apparently, like her 'lock up the negative thoughts' theory, you also had to clear your mind of negative thoughts to make room for the positive ones.

'"Negative thoughts glue themselves together until they have created a nasty ugly mess,"' Elise read.

'That sounds like Josh Gurney,' I told her. 'How am I supposed to get rid of him?'

She turned a page. '"Remind yourself that nothing is impossible".'

'Apart from getting taller.'

'*That's* why we're reading this book in the

first place! To make you taller! You have to believe in it, Anzo!'

'Sorry.' I'd known Elise for long enough to know that once she'd made up her mind, nothing would change it. If there was a gale-force wind blowing at Elise and she'd decided to stand in its way, I'd bet on her, not the wind.

'Did you do some chanting this morning?' she asked as we walked through the school gates.

'Yes, Mum.'

She raised her eyebrows. 'Very funny.' She held the book up to me. 'We'll concentrate on the other chapters after school. There's more to do.'

I caught sight of Miss Bentley across the playground. 'You're right,' I said. 'There is.'

* * *

There are probably lots of things worse than a rehearsal for *Snow White and the Seven Dwarfs* when you are playing all seven dwarfs, but that afternoon I was struggling to think of them. For a start, every time Miss Bentley said 'Grumpy', 'Sneezy', 'Dopey', 'Sleepy', 'Happy', 'Bashful' or 'Doc', everyone looked at me and sniggered. And since she was saying one of those seven names quite a lot, that made for a lot of sniggering. I tried to tune out and do some silent chanting.

I want to be tall, I want to be tall, I want to be tall . . .

But every time the sniggering seemed to be about to stop Josh made some whispered joke about Dopey or Grumpy and everyone started up again. In the end, Miss Bentley had to give her Morale-Raising speech. She didn't usually have to give this speech until really near the day of the actual play, so it showed that things had got desperate at an early stage. When Miss Bentley gave a speech she did a lot of hair flicking and pressed her hand to her chest as if she was in pain (though it was possible that talking to a crowd of kids from Froglets and Frogs was *actually* painful – it definitely was if she had Josh in her sights).

'Children,' she said, 'may I remind you that we are acting in this play for the joy of being on the stage?'

'Yeah, right,' I whispered to Elise. Elise, by the way, had been cast as 'Mirror'. This meant she got to stand behind a mirror and not be seen while Sonia Sesay pranced about in front of it saying, 'Mirror, mirror, on the wall, who is the fairest of them all?' Elise only had three lines to learn. I had about seven million.

That was the thing with Elise. She had the gift of being lucky. She kept telling me that you had to think lucky to be lucky, but I don't know how to *think lucky* any more than I know how to *think positive*.

Miss Bentley was pressing her hand to her chest, which meant we were getting to the most dramatic bit of her speech.

'If you laugh,' she said, in an urgent tone of voice that would have been perfect if she'd been telling us that there was a fire raging just behind us, 'if your attention wanders, if you don't give *one hundred per cent* of your commitment to this show, you are not just letting me down, you are not just letting your school down, you are letting *yourselves* down,' she told us. Her eyes squinted and she clutched the top button of her shirt as if just the *thought* of this mass let-down was causing her deep pain.

It probably was. Miss Bentley had been in charge of the school play for the last three years now. Every single year it had been a disaster. (You know it's bad when quite a lot of the school asks *not* to be in it.) The first year it was *The Wind in the Willows*. Miss Bentley had wanted to have four performances, but after the first night, when Toad drank too much Fanta before going on and belched his way through his lines, our head teacher decided that one performance was 'quite enough'. The year after that it was *Sleeping Beauty*, and Hazel Gardiner, who was playing the princess, actually did fall asleep (to be fair, people kept forgetting their lines so there were a lot of long gaps). The prince ended up having to *shout* her awake instead of just kissing her. Then last year Miss Bentley thought that maybe a musical would change the school's luck and she chose *Oliver!* But putting on a musical at All Stars was a *terrible* idea. You see, practically no one at our school can sing. I know there are people who think that everyone can perform, given time and help, but trust me, they haven't been to All Stars Primary School. (The name of the school is very misleading.) Also, since everyone knew that the majority of the school couldn't sing, the few people who *could* kept their mouths shut, probably because it was too much like hard work to stay in tune against a wave of wrong notes.

The singing was so bad that Miss Bentley spent most of the rehearsal time re-casting. In the end, five different sets of parents arrived on the night of the show thinking their son was playing the lead. After the performance some of the parents asked for their money back – even though the tickets were being sold as a fundraiser. (Maria Lightfoot's dad said he didn't want 'to contribute money towards that kind of catastrophe ever happening again'.)

So now you understand why Miss Bentley hasn't expressed any more interest in putting on musicals.

Each year Miss Bentley's speeches have become a bit more dramatic. Last year she even cried a bit. Everyone knew that this year's show was Miss Bentley's last chance. The head had apparently warned her that if this performance didn't show an improvement, then she was going to cancel all future dramatic productions and put the money towards a new IT suite instead.

Miss Bentley was standing up straighter now. She'd got to the part of the talk where she tried to make us feel enthusiastic about the show. In this bit of her speech she swapped pressing her hand to her chest for lots of hair flicking. 'This is going to be a lovely, funny, moving play,' she said.

'It's going to be funny all right – it's got Peanut in it!' Josh called out. There was another eruption of laughter. I exchanged a look with Elise, sending her my 'Why Does He Have to Be in My Life?' expression. She sent a look back – 'Eventually He Will Go Away.' Then she tapped at her forehead. This was her way of reminding me about one of her therapeutic techniques. Apparently if you tap at some of the 'pressure points' in your body (which are all in random places like your forehead and your wrists) then it makes you feel calm and able to deal with problems better. I'd tried it a few times but I can't say that tapping my forehead had ever made me feel better about dealing with Josh.

'Josh, that sort of comment is not helpful,' Miss Bentley said.

'Sorry, miss,' Josh said. 'I was only joking. I didn't mean to upset Anzo, honestly.' He made his eyes go big and round and sad. Have I mentioned that grown-ups thought Josh was really sweet? Even though he was basically Dr Slime, he had a way of looking like an angel whenever he needed to. Of course Miss Bentley fell for it.

'That's all right, Josh,' she said, giving him the kind of smile you'd give to a baby hamster. 'Just remember that we must be careful of other people's feelings.'

That's typical grown-up behaviour right there. Miss Bentley wasn't being careful of other people's feelings when she cast me as all seven dwarfs, was she?

* * *

'So what else is in this book besides the chanting?' We were walking in the playground, and the memory of Josh's face peering down at me just before our first rehearsal finished was still haunting me.

'Hey, Peanut, I think they forgot one of the other dwarf names,' he'd stage-whispered so that Miss Bentley didn't hear him but everyone else did. 'Wasn't there one called *Stumpy*?' Then he'd laughed his milkshake-slurping laugh and everyone else (apart from me and Elise) had laughed with him. If I'd been Giant, I would have picked him up and put him on top of the netball hoop and left him there overnight.

'It says you have to remove all negative thoughts from your head,' Elise said as we rounded the corner.

'You've been saying that for ages.'

'Yes, it's a common psychological technique,' Elise said. Sometimes she sounds forty-five instead of nearly twelve. 'But it also says you have to open yourself up to positive beginnings.'

'It's the positive *endings* I'm interested in,' I told her. 'Like me getting taller.'

'Just add it into your daily routine,' Elise told me. 'Like washing your face or brushing your teeth.'

I was a bit surprised she didn't write it on a Post-it note.

Not Everyone
Is Josh Gurney

In case you think I was always miserable at school, I'm going to tell you about art. I mean art at school, not art in general (that would take way too long, and besides, I'm not sure an extensive knowledge of Snoopy, Calvin and Hobbes and the Marvel comics counts). Art was my favourite subject, which is maybe not all that surprising given that I loved drawing cartoons and making comics. Ms Brown taught us art and was my favourite teacher, not just because of the art but because she wasn't always making references to my height. Even when the other teachers were nice about it, they couldn't help being nice about it in a way that made me even more aware of it. For instance, we might be doing a project on Romans and making a model of a Roman soldier out of papier mâché and chicken wire (every single project we've ever done with Mr Dooley has been made out of papier mâché and chicken wire) and Mr Dooley would need something from one of the higher shelves. He'd say 'Anzo, could you reach up and –' and then he'd stop and look at me and say, 'I'm sorry, how thoughtless. Of course you can't. Never mind.' It was stuff like this that kept me feeling that no matter what Elise, Liam and a few others said, what I looked like *did* make a difference to how everyone treated me. I didn't want to be talked down to, in more ways than one.

But in art Ms Brown never asked anyone to fetch anything. She let us sit and get on with our projects, coming round to us one at a time and giving us advice. She also arranged the desks in a way that meant that I never sat near Josh and his followers. Instead, I was at a table with Elise, Liam, Celia Wanstead and Finn Achebe. They were the ones who never laughed along with the milkshake-slurper Josh and who never, ever called me Peanut. While we were drawing and painting, we usually talked about the Marvel films and what superpower we'd have.

'I'd have flying, definitely,' Liam said. 'I mean, even if you're in trouble, you can always get away, right?'

'I'd have invisibility,' Celia said. 'If they can't see you, they can't get you.'

'I'd be made of rubber,' said Finn. 'Then I could bounce over whatever was trying to get me.'

'I'd be a giant,' I said. 'Then I could squash anyone who was after me.'

Elise raised her eyebrows. 'You realise you all have some serious issues, right?'

'Being a superhero is all about winning over the bad guys, Elise,' Liam said.

'I thought it was about helping people,' Elise said.

I heard Josh's milkshake laugh from across the room and we all exchanged a glance.

'Yeah, but *first* it's about winning over the bad guys,' Finn said.

If we'd had art every day, I don't think I would have minded All Stars too much.

The Power of Reading

'**A**ha! It's wee Anzo, is it?' Dad shouted as I came into the kitchen for dinner.

I didn't say anything because I knew he wasn't expecting a reply. It was just a kick-start for one of my family's performances. I smiled and sat down to watch the show.

Uncle Talbert grinned. 'You're not calling that a Scottish accent, are you?'

And they were off.

Dad drew his eyebrows up and squared his shoulders as if he was a bouncer at a nightclub. He stared at Uncle Talbert in mock outrage. 'Are you questioning my abilities as an actor?'

'Yes!' Uncle Talbert reached over and grabbed Dad's cheek, pinching it as if Dad was a baby.

Dad smacked Uncle Talbert's hand away and

turned to Mum. 'My own love, my darling, save me from these cretins who don't know a Scottish accent from a haggis in a haggis tree!'

Mum laughed. 'You don't need saving, you need shutting up.' She walked over to him and bumped him with her hip. He turned to smile at her, slipping his arm around her waist. I know a lot of people my age might hate seeing their parents go gooey over each other, but I liked it. Uncle Talbert started an impersonation of a romantic violin playing just behind Mum and Dad's heads.

'Get out of it,' Dad told him. He turned to me. 'He's just jealous, you know. That I've got the love of your beautiful mother.'

'Oh, stop,' Mum said.

I thought about trying to join in the conversation. Maybe telling them about how Ms Brown had said I was 'really coming along with my perspective work' in art. Or how Elise had told me that she thought my latest comic was my best yet, better even than *Giant Versus Dr Slime*. But I felt myself go all hot again as I tried to think of the best and funniest way to put it and by then Uncle Talbert was already fake crying about not having the love of a good woman like my mother and Uncle Miles had appeared in the doorway.

'SIT DOWN, ALL,' Uncle Miles roared as he carried a big pot over to the table and set it down. 'PREPARE TO HAVE YOUR TASTE BUDS DELIGHTED. THIS IS THE BEST VEGETARIAN CHILLI IN THE WORLD.' He waved a serving spoon like a conductor's baton. 'It's going to be a central dish at our restaurant. Obviously.'

Uncle Talbert immediately stopped the fake crying and launched into a story about a chilli he was once served in a back room in Mexico where the bartender challenged him to eat ten helpings in one sitting. 'I could have fuelled a space rocket with those farts!'

Everyone collapsed into giggles. As I looked round the table I thought how good it was to be part of this family – how funny they were, how they always had stories to tell.

How was I ever going to measure up to them?

* * *

That night I chanted, 'I want to be tall,' about seven hundred times. To be honest, it might not actually have been seven hundred times, but it was a *lot*. I also tried to picture myself as tall, and every time a negative thought came into my head (usually involving Josh), I tried to push it out. I wanted to be more like the rest of my family, and that meant growing. Being tall helped them to be sure and clear about everything they felt and wanted. Being tall meant they never, ever had to get nervous about speaking in front of people. People looked up to you when you were tall – in both senses.

Over the next week or so I got in the habit of chanting every chance I got. There was something weirdly soothing about the words.

Iwanttobetall I want to be tall I wanttobe tall . . .

It was like a little rhythmic drum in my head.

Iwanttobetall I want to be tall I wanttobe tall . . .

And I discovered that if I chanted in my head when Josh was around, I could almost tune him out.

* * *

Then one morning I was brushing my teeth (*I want to be tall I wanttobe tall . . .*) when I realised something. I'd opened the door of the wall cabinet in the bathroom, where the toothbrushes and toothpaste were kept, without stretching. I stood for a second trying to think. Was I misremembering the height of the cabinet? Maybe Mum had moved it as part of a DIY project. I went out to the hall and shouted down the stairs.

'MUM?' (In case you think I was being rude, you should know that yelling in this house isn't bad manners, it's the only way to communicate. If you don't shout, no one hears you.) 'MUM?'

'WHAT IS IT?' There was a bang downstairs as she dropped something heavy onto the floor. Probably her drill. She was the only person I'd ever heard of who stuck a drill in the pocket of their dressing gown – just in case.

'DID YOU MOVE THE BATHROOM CABINET?'

'NO.'

'OK, THANKS.'

I went back into the bathroom and reached up to the cabinet. I could definitely reach the handle without going on tiptoes. Mum hadn't lowered the cabinet. It could only mean one thing.

I raced to my room. This was it. This was where I'd find out the truth. On the back of the door were pencil marks showing my height from when I was five years old and convinced that I would be as tall as Mum and Dad any day, to the one when I finally decided not to depress myself by measuring myself any more.

I turned around and backed up against the door, resting a pencil on top of my head. I pushed the pencil back and wiggled it, so I could be sure I'd made a mark. Then I took another deep breath and turned round.

I'd grown.

I'd grown!

All right, I was still technically very, very short. But I was a very, very tiny bit *less* short than I had been.

* * *

That morning I chanted 'I want to be tall' two hundred and seventy-four times before I went to school. It would have been two hundred and seventy-five except that Elise called round for me because I was late calling round for her.

'I've grown!' I said as soon as I came out of the house.

'Wait. Stand still.' Elise took a step back and squinted at me. She gave a slightly doubtful nod. 'Yeah, maybe.'

'No, not maybe. Definitely.' I told her about the back of the door.

'So *The Power of Positive Thinking* works?' She sounded shocked.

'Didn't you think it would?' I mean, I had to admit that *I* hadn't really thought it would, but I'd assumed Elise had. She was lucky. She was positive. She believed in things. She made people feel better. And now it looked like she made wishes come true as well.

Elise pushed one of her bracelets further up her arm. 'I hoped so, but . . .' Then she turned to me and grinned. 'This is great!'

'I know.' I was already thinking about the number of chants I could fit in that evening.

Elise started walking really fast. 'So if you keep up the chanting and the visualisations and keep your mind clear of negative thoughts, you could be . . . well, you could be a lot taller soon! Think how happy you'll feel then!'

I couldn't wait.

Inching Upwards

Of course, no one else noticed I'd grown, because when you're as short as I was it takes more than a few millimetres to make a real difference. Josh was now calling me 'Stumpy' – which seemed to be the replacement name for 'Peanut'. Stumpy was not an improvement. It almost made me miss the days of being a nut.

* * *

Meanwhile, in rehearsals, Miss Bentley was trying to teach me seven accents so that my dwarfs would all sound different.

It turned out I was not good at accents. My

Australian sounded Swedish and my French sounded like Russian. After a while, even my own accent didn't sound all that convincing. What worried me was that Miss Bentley didn't seem to care. She kept saying 'Good, good,' whatever came out of my mouth.

She'd decided to put cardboard cut-outs of each of the seven dwarfs onstage. Her idea was that when I stood in front of each one, that dwarf would become 'live'. She said we could increase the potential for comedy by having me jump from dwarf to dwarf. When I got to the relevant cut-out, I could change my accent and mannerisms for each one. I tried telling Miss Bentley that I didn't think my acting skills were up to it, but she didn't seem to hear me.

'Come on, Anzo, let's see your best efforts. Practise your moves between the cut-outs.'

I did try. Maybe I shouldn't have. Because my best efforts made her happy but gave me a sense of impending doom and everyone else a fit of hysterics.

'This production will be a comic triumph,' she told me.

What she meant was that everyone would laugh so hard at me that the performance would be a huge success, wipe out all memories of previous productions and she'd be allowed to stay in charge of the school play.

Which is why I was now resting all my hopes on *The Power of Positive Thinking* and the few millimetres I'd grown so far. All I had to do was keep going.

* * *

I'd hoped for overnight success. I increased my chanting every night until the words 'I want to be tall' sounded like a tap dance in my head. But it wasn't until two weeks later that it began to be noticeable. Every morning I'd measure myself, and although it didn't always look like I'd grown much, over the course of each week it was clear I had. Millimetre by millimetre, I was getting taller.

'You've grown such a lot,' Elise said one morning. 'Maybe you shouldn't do quite so much chanting.'

'Elise! I want to be taller! Not two inches taller – a *lot* taller!' I couldn't believe what she was saying. 'I thought you'd be pleased!'

'I am, I am,' Elise said. She reached out and tugged at my arm, her bracelets jangling. 'But you don't want to grow *too* quickly. You might put your bones under stress.'

Because of her mum and dad, Elise knew all kinds of things about health and development. But sometimes she would tell you things you didn't really want to know. Like you'd be about to eat a burger and she'd tell you how the body processed saturated fats – which was interesting – but not something I really wanted to think about while I was *actually* in the process of processing them. So I wasn't in the mood now to find out that growing quickly wasn't a one-hundred-per-cent good thing. As far as I was concerned, there was absolutely no downside to growing as much as possible in the shortest possible time. I wanted to be tall enough to look Josh in his stupid big brown eyes and tell him what I thought of him. I wanted to be tall enough to look *anyone* in the eyes.

Elise must have figured out from my expression what I was thinking because she nudged me again. 'Sorry. You're right. It's fantastic. I just didn't expect it to be so dramatic.'

'It's not that dramatic,' I said. 'Mum and Dad haven't even noticed.'

'But they don't notice anything—'

'About me?' I interrupted.

She gave me a funny look. 'No, Anzo. I meant, they don't notice anything apart from the restaurant.'

Which was kind of the same thing.

The End of the
Seven Dwarfs

It wasn't that much of a surprise when the first person apart from Elise to notice wasn't Mum and wasn't Dad and wasn't Uncle Miles or Uncle Talbert. It was Miss Bentley. When you cast the smallest person in Year 6 as all seven dwarfs and build the whole show around the 'comic' effect, you're probably going to notice if the dwarf has become almost as tall as Snow White.

During rehearsals one Wednesday after the Easter holidays, Miss Bentley called me over. 'Anzo, are you wearing different shoes?'

I shook my head. 'No.'

She frowned, as if I'd given her the wrong answer – which I guess, in her eyes, I had.

'Have you – *grown*?' She asked the question as if she was asking me if I'd committed a crime.

'Yes,' I said. 'I think I'm having a bit of a growth spurt.'

'I see.' Miss Bentley was quiet for what felt like a long time. I could almost hear what she was thinking.

Oh no, not another Oliver!

'Well,' she said in a brighter voice, flicking her hair back in a put-a-brave-face-on-it way, 'I'm sure it won't continue. Children don't just *keep* growing like that.'

'Isn't that the point about children?' I said. 'That they're growing?'

Miss Bentley flushed. 'Well, yes, of course, but they don't just go from being a . . . being very . . . uh . . .' A little line appeared between her eyebrows. 'I mean, children – people – don't grow that *quickly*, I mean. But in the meantime, perhaps you could bend your knees a little when you're onstage? Just so that you still look – just so that you still really fit the part?'

'OK.' By that point I wasn't worried about *Snow White and the Seven Dwarfs* any more. I trusted *The Power of Positive Thinking*. I trusted my chant (*I want to be tall, I want to be tall,*

Iwanttobetall . . .). I trusted that it was only a matter of time before Miss Bentley would have to take action.

* * *

It was almost half-term (and another three inches later) before it happened though. By that time Miss Bentley was a nervous wreck. Every time she saw me the little line between her eyes got longer and deeper. It was probably growing at the same rate as I was. She finally cracked two days before we broke up for the holidays.

'Anzo? May I talk to you for a moment?'

I felt bad for her in a way. It was true she'd worked really hard to make the play a good comedy. But then again, she'd worked really hard to make me the joke.

'This might make you feel upset, Anzo,' Miss Bentley said. 'But sometimes in show business, well . . .'

I decided to make it a bit easier for her. 'The show has to go on *without* you?'

Her eyebrows shot up. 'Oh, I see you – Um, yes, the thing is, when I cast you, you were, uh, perfect for the roles. But now that you've had such a growth spurt . . .'

'I'm not the best choice for the seven dwarfs any more. That's all right.'

The little line between her eyes smoothed away. 'You don't mind?'

'No,' I said. I thought about telling her that being the laughing stock of the school (again) wasn't one of my educational goals but I decided that sometimes it's best to keep your mouth shut.

'I mean, I know you were worried at first about appearing onstage, but lately in rehearsals it's really felt like you've been enjoying yourself.'

And she was right, I had. I'd stopped worrying about being in the play because I knew sooner or later I *wouldn't* be. I'd concentrated on chanting in my head when Josh was in sight, and having a laugh with Elise and Liam (who'd come in late to the show as the huntsman). It had been a laugh, but now I was happy it was over.

'Honestly, it's fine,' I said. 'Maybe I could help out backstage or something instead.'

'Anzo, that's very big of you,' Miss Bentley said, with the nicest smile I'd ever seen her give me, like she really meant it. Then she let out a high-pitched giggle. 'Ooh, did you hear what I said? Big of you!' she said, giggling again. 'That's funny.'

I didn't laugh. I was too busy processing what she'd said. Her calling me 'big' wasn't funny because I *wasn't* big, it was because I *was*.

Another thought struck me. Before I'd started growing, at last once a week one of the teachers would accidentally call me 'Peanut'. That hadn't happened in weeks.

'Anzo? Do you feel OK?' Miss Bentley was peering at me, the line back between her eyes.

I grinned at her. 'Yes. I feel fine.' I felt more than fine. I felt *tall*.

Miss Bentley ended up casting seven boys from Year 1 as the dwarfs and cutting their lines to almost nothing. All they had to do was come onstage and basically look cute. They didn't even have to learn any accents.

The End of
Stumpy and Peanut

It took another inch before my parents finally noticed what was happening to me.

'So, Anzo, you've entered the growing phase,' Uncle Talbert said one evening.

'Yeah, I—'

'Looks like you'll be overtaking us soon,' Uncle Miles plonked a big casserole dish down on the table and gestured for everyone to sit down.

'It was—' I started. But no one heard me.

'I hope not,' Dad said, helping himself to a plate. 'He needs to be at least twenty-one before he overtakes me in anything. Otherwise world order will be destroyed.'

'Rubbish,' said Uncle Talbert. 'He'll be better than you in all areas. Not that *that* will be hard.'

'Oi!'

Mum laughed. 'Growth spurts are funny,' she said.'I remember when I got tall. My grandmother was convinced it was all down to me eating so many apples.'

Uncle Miles threw his arms out wide. 'There you are! Anzo's growing because of my FABULOUS cooking!'

'Is *that* what we're calling burned sausages these days?' Dad asked.

Mum laughed. 'Don't you take any notice of him, Miles,' she said. 'Your cooking is delicious. That's why we're investing our whole future in it.'

Then the conversation moved on to how old all of them had been when *they* had first become tall, and what they'd been eating at the time, and whether Uncle Miles was a good cook who was just having an unfortunate run of bad luck when it came to pork.

I sat there listening and realised that what they were saying was that they hadn't always been exceptionally tall. That they had all gone through a sudden growth spurt like me. That my growing taller probably had nothing to do with my chanting. And that I still wasn't involved in their conversation. Even though my mouth

was a lot nearer their ears, they still couldn't
seem to hear me.

* * *

For a while, school was the one thing that *was*
better. I wish I could have taken a photo of
Josh's face the day that he called me 'Stumpy'
and Celia Wanstead turned around and said, 'But
Anzo *isn't* stumpy now, is he, Josh?'

Josh scowled, but he couldn't say anything
because Celia Wanstead was right.

So that was the end of 'Stumpy' and 'Peanut'.

I would have liked to spend more time
celebrating that particular development, but Elise
was still worrying about me. She'd started
entering my measurements on a chart and
muttering about speed and strain.

'I don't know why you're worrying,' I said.
'It's not like I've got any control over it.' I'd
explained about my family's history of growing
in the same way, and she'd admitted that after
talking to her mum she'd suspected that the
chanting might not have had that much to do
with me getting taller. (It turned out that Elise's
mum and dad thought chanting was only helpful
for 'creating a positive mindset' and that it was

unlikely to actually change you physically –
though Elise was keeping an open mind.)
Although I still found '*I want to be tall*' going
round in my head sometimes, it was more from
habit than anything else. The fact was, I was
growing whether I chanted or not.

'I'm just worried it's happening so fast,' Elise
said. 'I don't want you to be unhealthy.'

'I am healthy,' I said. 'I'm just growing a bit.'

But the thing was, as the weeks went on,
it became obvious that I wasn't just growing a
bit – I was growing *a lot*.

* * *

For a while, there was so much to love about
being tall.

No one called me 'Shorty', 'Stumpy' or
'Peanut' any more. They called me 'Anzo' or,
even better, 'All right?' 'All right' was what the
cool kids got. 'All right' meant acceptance. 'All
right' meant I was not a freak.

There were other things too.

I didn't have to go on tiptoes to open
cupboards.

Bus drivers stopped saying, 'Oh, hello – nearly
missed you down there.'

I was never missed in the head counts on coach trips.

Josh stopped using me as an armrest.

When Elise and I walked down the street, people didn't assume I was her baby brother.

For a while, being taller was everything I'd dreamed it would be.

The Golden Ticket

When the second envelope from the International Cartoon Strip Association arrived, I thought it must be a brochure for some of the training courses they ran. I figured that getting an Honourable Mention must have put me on their mailing list. Just the thought that I was on their mailing list made me feel good. To me the International Cartoon Strip Association was a bit like royalty.

But the envelope wasn't a brochure, it was an invitation. An invitation to attend their Comic Con. And because I'd won an Honourable Mention in their last competition, they were offering me a fifty-per-cent discount off the cost of going.

I scanned the letter – the convention would

take place over two days. The schedule included workshops and talks about drawing techniques, an exhibition of original Marvel comics and a Q&A with the professional cartoonist Jesse Edward (Jesse Edward was definite royalty – he'd drawn for some of the biggest names in the cartoon business! He was a legend). There was even a special cartoon competition for all the people who attended. As trips went, this had to be the best I'd ever heard of. It was *definitely* better than rock-pooling. But the hotel where the Comic Con was taking place was two hundred and fifty miles away and even with fifty per cent off, it would cost money. I folded up the letter and put it in my pocket. Amazing, yes. Possible, no. Not unless I could turn into Giant for real.

I wandered through to what Dad called 'The Site of Opportunity' – in other words, the dining bit of the restaurant-to-be. Mum had knocked down the wall between our old living room and dining room to make the main restaurant (we now ate in the kitchen and watched television in the spare room upstairs) and had been plastering the new walls for the last week. Now it wasn't just clouds of flour that you walked into when you opened the front door, it was clouds of plaster dust too. For a few days even Dad, Uncle Miles and Uncle Talbert stopped talking as much in case they got a mouthful. Though my family even seemed to cough louder than anyone else.

There was one problem with their big plan, and that was that they couldn't decide on the restaurant's name. When I came in, they were having yet another talk about it. It was going as well as it usually did – badly.

'It's the thing we've always wanted to do, so we should call it "Heart's Desire",' Uncle Miles was saying as I perched on a rung of Mum's stepladder. 'I mean, it's taken us long enough to be able to do it.'

Uncle Talbert snorted. 'It should be something about the stomach, not the heart. It should be about food!'

'I suppose you want to call it "Stomach's Desire".' Uncle Miles screwed up his face. 'You have no poetry in your soul. That's why you're not a chef. The restaurant name should have some poetry, some finesse, some class.'

'How about "Tuck in Tommy's"? That's alliterative, so there's the poetry. And it does what it says on the tin – it's clearly a restaurant. Job done.' Uncle Talbert held out his arms – *Ta-da*.

'My. Name. Is. Not. Tommy.' You could practically see the steam coming out of Uncle Miles's ears. 'And we are not going to be running a restaurant where people *tuck in*.'

'What will they be doing then?' Uncle Talbert looked genuinely bewildered. He turned to Dad for help.

Dad grinned. Dad was usually the one to sort out the fights between Uncle Miles and Uncle Talbert, but I think he liked to watch them for a while first. It was like a bit of entertaining telly to him.

'They will be *relishing, savouring* and *appreciating* my genius cooking skills!' Uncle Miles brandished a wooden spoon at Uncle Talbert as if he wanted to duel with him. (He always had a cooking utensil in his hand the same way Mum always had a hammer or a drill.)

'All right then. How about just "Tasty Tuck"?' Uncle Talbert said.

Uncle Miles spluttered dramatically.

'What? What did I say?'

'Maybe we need to give this a bit more thought,' Dad said. 'I don't think the two of you are quite on the same page.'

'We're not even in the same book.' Uncle Miles sniffed.

'What about "Time for Dinner" but with "time" spelled like the herb, you know, "t-h-y-m-e",' Mum said.

'It sounds like a children's book,' Uncle Miles said grumpily. You could tell he was getting into one of his tempers, the same kind he got into when he made cheese sauce too fast and it went lumpy.

'Maybe you could name the restaurant after one of your signature dishes,' I said.

Dad laughed. 'I don't think you should get involved, Anzo – we've already got more than enough opinions muddying the waters. You're best off staying out of it.'

Maybe Dad meant it as a joke, but what he'd said was exactly the problem – I was out of it. And apparently that's where I was going to stay.

Same Old Story

When I'd dreamed of being taller, I'd always imagined that as soon as I got bigger Josh would stop pestering me because he'd have nothing to pester me about any more. While I was a size somewhere between tiny and normal, that had been more or less true. Or at least his attempts to find names for me hadn't been so successful. But now that my height was becoming obvious in a different way, Josh was finding other material.

Did you notice that I said 'other' material, not 'new'?

'Hey, how's the weather up there?' he said one morning when I walked into the classroom.

Even though this is the same question that idiots have been asking tall people for about fifty-five billion years, a few people sniggered.

A snigger to Josh is like a drop of blood to a piranha fish.

He glanced around him and then back up at me. 'Yeah, how does it feel to be a street lamp?'

There are some people who would have been able to come up with a really funny reply to what he'd said. Like in films where the hero is being taunted by the enemy and then manages to turn everything around with one clever, funny remark that gets everyone on the hero's side.

But the thing is, those films were written by people who had spent months coming up with that clever, funny remark. I had about two seconds.

I stared down at him and hoped that me being so much taller than him would make him put a sock in it.

But he just grinned up at me and then looked round to collect his extra sniggers. I could see that he was back to what he was before I'd started growing. It was like all the attention he was getting was making *him* grow.

* * *

At first I'd been really pleased that my growing spurt didn't show any signs of stopping. But now I was starting to realise the truth of the phrase 'too much of a good thing'.

The first time I bumped my head on a doorway it was funny – I was even happy about it. It proved I wasn't short any more! But then it kept happening. Everywhere. Entering classrooms, getting on buses, even coming into my bedroom.

Then there was the fact that suddenly I had to sit at the back of the classroom all the time because my head blocked the view of the board (not that anyone except the teachers minded). These days it was hard to fit my legs under my desk, so I had to sit sideways or squeeze them underneath so that the desk scraped the tops of my knees. Being tall was starting to mean being bruised.

The back was where Josh sat, so suddenly he could get at me *all the time*. There are only so many jokes about Jack and the Beanstalk (featuring me as the giant – or the beanstalk) that any person can hear in one day. None was about my limit.

Then there was PE. Because I was not a lucky person like Elise, this term it was athletics. Not only athletics – long jump. According to some people (everyone), people who have long legs will be good at long jump. The problem was, my legs didn't seem to understand what was expected of them. If body parts can be stupid, my legs were really dumb.

'Come on, Anzo, give us a *real* jump! Use your beanpoles!' Nathan decided to chime in while I was standing in line waiting for my turn.

Nathan was one of Josh's friends, which meant he wasn't one of mine. It was easy to be a friend of Josh's. All you had to do was laugh whenever you got your cue (Josh's milkshake laugh) and pick on the people Josh had decided to pick on for the day (usually me).

'Come on, use your beanpoles!' Nathan said again. The thing about Josh and his friends is that when they find a joke, they stick to it like superglue. If they feel they've hit on the winning formula, they will repeat it until every last drop of humour has been got out of it. Unfortunately for the rest of us, that to them appears to be never.

'You're up,' Josh told me helpfully, as if being tall had impaired my vision of Liam walking away from the long jump ahead. Liam gave me a thumbs-up as I took my place and I could see Finn waving encouragement from behind Josh's leering face. Elise was smiling her 'Go Get 'Em' smile, which she usually gave me when the situation was hopeless.

Like I said, you'd think that having substantially longer legs would make for a substantially longer long jump. But in my case, it didn't. Short or long, my legs were not my friends. Mr Dooley confirmed it as soon as I'd had my turn.

'Never mind, Anzo, you've just got to grow into them,' he called out.

I think he meant it nicely but, everyone (well, Josh and Nathan and a couple of the girls) thought it was hysterically funny.

It looked like my size was *always* going to be a problem – too short or too tall, it was what stood between me and 'All right'.

With a Little Help from Your Friends

In our next art lesson I told Elise, Liam and Finn about the Comic Con invitation.

And then wished I hadn't.

'But you've got to go!' Elise's bracelets sounded like they were about to leap off her arms with excitement. 'It sounds fantastic!'

'It's two hundred and fifty miles away,' I told her.

Elise stared at me. 'You've been invited to go to a conference on your favourite thing in the whole world and you're saying you can't because it's a train ride away.'

'You should definitely go.' Liam leaned over. 'You might meet one of the people who works for Marvel and they could give you a job.'

'In case you haven't noticed, I'm not a grown-up,' I said. 'And I'm at school.'

Liam shrugged. 'Yeah, but now you're really tall, you kind of *look* like a grown-up.'

Elise swivelled round to look at me, her eyes lighting up. 'He does, doesn't he?'

I looked at them, assuming it was a joke – but none of them were laughing. All this time I'd been about the same height as a skirting board, and now they were saying I could pass as a grown-up?

'Yeah.' Finn nodded. 'My mum was telling me about this comedian guy who started selling jokes when he was, like, thirteen or something. He just did it after school or while he was having breakfast. He got really famous.'

'What's his name?' Liam asked.

Finn shrugged. 'I don't know. I mean, he's famous to old people, not to us.'

'Anzo could definitely draw cartoons for Marvel. Look at how good this is,' Liam pointed to the poster I was doing for *Snow White*. I'd made the dwarfs into little superheroes with capes and given Snow White some serious muscles. She looked like she could take on Spider-Man. I didn't know what Miss Bentley would make of it, but Ms Brown had called it 'tremendously inventive'.

'So if you don't go,' Elise said, 'you'll be missing the chance of starting your career in your chosen field.'

'I really don't think going to the Comic Con is going to mean I get a job.'

Elise raised one eyebrow. (Did I mention she can do that? She can also flare her nostrils and waggle her ears. She's really very talented.) Then she gave me her 'Quoting from a Book' look. 'People who believe things happen discover that things happen.'

'Have you actually memorised *The Power of Positive Thinking*?'

'No. I've just paid very close attention to it. You should too.'

'Forget about the job bit,' Finn said. 'You should go because it would be a laugh.'

'Yeah, you'd be able to hang out with lots of other people who like drawing capes.' Liam punched me in the arm and laughed.

'My family won't agree to it anyway,' I said. 'They're really busy with the restaurant and they're not going to let me go on my own, are they? Plus it costs money.'

'First, you haven't even asked them yet,' Elise said. 'And second, you get a discount, remember?'

'You should at least ask, mate,' Finn said.

Liam nodded. 'What's the worst that can happen?'

I've never liked that phrase. Generally I don't want to find out the worst that can happen. Because sometimes it does.

'Promise you'll ask,' Elise said.

There was no question mark on the end of her sentence.

Sometimes I'd Rather Be Wrong Than Be Right

I thought that maybe if I tried at dinner time, I might have a better chance. Out of the four of them, one of them would have to think it was a good idea, right?

Wrong.

'A *convention*? But why would you want to go to a *convention*?' Dad said. 'Believe me, Anzo, conventions are deadly dull. I've had to go to a few myself and they're all talk, talk, talk.'

'And that's just him,' Uncle Talbert said.

'Ha ha,' Dad said. 'Your wit is marshmallow sharp as usual.'

Mum was helping herself to some more of

Uncle Miles's new 'signature' dish – butter beans with apples, celery, beetroot and peanuts. 'And it's so far away, Anzo. One of us would have to take you and I've only just started putting the new kitchen counters in.'

'Which isn't making cooking any easier,' Uncle Miles told her. 'I don't know how you expect me to produce culinary wonders without a proper work surface.'

'So *that's* what you call this,' Dad said, pointing at the signature dish. 'A "culinary wonder". Well, I guess it is a wonder how you decided these ingredients went together . . .'

'That is no way to speak to the chef of our restaurant. You need my imagination.'

'Sure we do,' Dad said. 'Maybe just not quite so much of it.'

Uncle Miles sniffed as if he was offended, but I saw him wink at Mum. Uncle Miles isn't easily offended unless he's in a bad mood. Maybe because he and Dad and Uncle Talbert are always competing with each other and trading insults, they've developed thick skins. I wondered why I'd never managed that, even though Josh had been calling me names for the last six years.

It was all getting off-topic.

'It's not that far by train,' I said, my voice quieter than I wanted it to be.

'It's probably a scam,' Uncle Talbert said. 'They'll get you there and then charge you the earth for everything.'

'Everything's included in the ticket price, and I get a big discount,' I said. 'I thought maybe the rest could be my birthday and Christmas present,' I said, turning to Mum and Dad. 'And I've got a bit saved up from birthdays and . . .' But I didn't get to finish because Uncle Talbert had picked up the letter I'd brought to the table and tossed it back to me.

'Believe me, Anzo, it won't be worth it. You're not really fussed about going anyway, are you? I mean, I know you liked cartoons when you were little, but that was years ago.'

I stared at him. He didn't even remember the Snoopy book.

Mum leaned over and patted my hand. 'You probably feel like you *should* go, don't you? Don't worry, these organisations send invitations to hundreds of people and they probably offer everyone "the discount"' – she did quotes in the air with her fingers – 'to make them feel they're getting a special deal. They won't mind if you don't turn up — they won't even notice. You shouldn't feel pushed to do something you don't really want to.'

I stared at her. She didn't even remember my Honourable Mention letter.

'But—' I said. I was going to try and explain, to tell them what it meant, what the International Cartoon Strip Association really was, when Dad broke in.

'Well, if you thought you should go just because they asked you, don't worry — we're all letting you off the hook. You don't have to go. There, sorted!' He clapped his hands and turned to Uncle Miles. 'Any chance of dessert?'

'Not just any dessert,' Uncle Miles said. 'Tonight's is special.'

Dad and Uncle Talbert immediately started trying to guess what it was ('Frogs' legs with ice cream!', 'Blueberry and broccoli trifle!') and they'd all moved on.

I jerked up out of my seat. 'Wait!'

They all turned to look at me and stopped talking, waiting. My skin and ears grew hot and my mouth dried.

'What's up, Anzo?' Uncle Miles said.

'Nothing,' I said. 'It's fine.'

I grabbed the letter from the table and stuffed it into my pocket. And then I went up to my room. I didn't even wait to find out what the dessert was.

Lonely in a Crowd

I didn't tell Elise about trying and failing to get Mum and Dad to agree to let me go. Maybe because I knew that Elise wouldn't have taken no for an answer if she'd been in my place. Maybe because she wouldn't understand why I hadn't explained to them that it was important to me. Maybe because I hadn't even told her that they didn't really know about my cartoons.

Most of all, because I didn't want to hear what she'd have to say (and I knew she'd have a *lot* to say).

More and more I was coming to understand that while I was even more visible than before to my enemies, I was still invisible to my family. Mum, Dad, Uncle Miles and Uncle Talbert – they didn't really know who I was at all.

All this time I'd thought that growing tall would make all my problems shrink. It turned out some of them were going to stay the size they'd always been.

* * *

When I heard Miss Bentley asking Ms Brown to organise the sets for *Snow White*, I went up to them straight away. 'Can I help?'

'It's a lot of work,' Ms Brown told me, looking a bit doubtful.

'I don't mind,' I told her. 'I can do it in lunchtimes and break times.'

'I think he'd really like to be involved in the show, now that he's not starring in it,' Miss Bentley said in a whisper that was louder than her ordinary speaking voice. She cocked her head at me, clearly thinking she was being sensitive and subtle. 'You know, it's been hard on him, giving up such a great part.'

Ms Brown looked over at me with a tucked-in smile and gave me a quick half wink. I think she knew that giving up my dwarf roles hadn't been hard on me at all. But she was really happy to have my help. It turned out she had volunteered to organise a community art project outside school and so she didn't have a lot of spare time. 'You'll be saving me a lot of stress, Anzo,' she told me.

She didn't realise she was saving me a lot of stress too. If Elise noticed something was wrong (and Elise noticed everything), then she'd start asking questions. I wasn't ready for her questions. The thing about Elise asking questions is that she usually already had the answers. And I definitely wasn't ready for those.

Painting the sets with Ms Brown was fun. She told me it was great that I'd volunteered to help because it was good to have someone tall enough to paint the tops.

'Some of us aren't so lucky in the height department,' she told me, smiling.

Standing next to her, I realised that Ms Brown wasn't all that tall for a grown-up. It was funny, I'd never thought of her as small before. It must have been her personality that made her seem bigger.

* * *

Between spending all my free time at school painting the sets and life at home being normal (everyone else loud and funny, me invisible), after a couple of days I realised I was feeling a bit lonely. It's weird how being around people who are all having a good time can make you feel more alone than if you were actually alone.

I started having trouble sleeping. I'd go to bed and my head would fill with thoughts about the conference and my latest cartoon. About Josh and his laugh and how he kept finding new names to call me (Giraffe, Big Bird, Skyscraper, Stretch). About my family and how I couldn't seem to find a way to talk to them. About Elise and how she'd gone to so much effort to try to help me be happy, only to see me stay miserable. One night I leaned over to my clock radio to see the time and decided to turn the radio on. It would be a voice to keep me company. That's when I discovered Night Owl Bob. Night Owl Bob was a DJ who had a late-night show. In between the songs he played, he invited people to call in to chat about whatever subject he'd decided on for that night's show. I liked it straight away. He did programmes about what an island in Scotland sounded like after dark, or people who had had their lives changed forever after getting a phone call in the middle of the night meant for someone else, or people who had unusual talents (there was a man who could drum with his feet, a woman who could whistle any tune but only backwards and another woman who could mimic any accent as soon as she heard it). I listened to it every night after that. There's something about late-night radio that gives the impression that you're part of a club. It feels like the place where lonely people get together.

That first night, Night Owl Bob's show was about dancing and he asked for people to call in with their thoughts and stories. One man named Mick called in. He was almost whispering, as if he was nervous of saying the wrong thing. But Night Owl Bob is good with people. He knows how to encourage them, to make his voice sound kind and welcoming, like he's an old friend inviting them to come in and sit down. It wasn't long before Mick relaxed and started to talk.

'I used to love going dancing,' he said. 'You'd laugh about me saying that if you saw me, because I'm built more for moving bricks than moving feet, but I loved it.'

'What kind of dancing did you do, Mick?' Night Owl Bob asked. Bob's voice sounds so soft you'd think it was made of cream cheese. It must be amazing to have a voice like that, a voice where when you speak, everyone wants to listen.

'All kinds really,' Mick said. He didn't sound nervous any more and you could hear how he was enjoying thinking about himself dancing. 'Bit of ballroom, bit of Latin. I even took some tap lessons once.'

'It sounds as if you loved it.'

There was a small sigh. 'I did, Bob, I did.'

'So why did you stop?'

There was a pause so long I thought that maybe they'd lost the call, but finally Mick started speaking again. His voice was speeded up this time, like someone was tapping a watch to show he didn't have long. He sounded small and sad.

'One night I went to this class. I'd been going for a while so I knew most of the people. They were a nice lot – liked to have a laugh, but liked to get on with the dancing too. There was this woman there. I'd not seen her before. When I walked in she was talking about all the competitions she'd been in, how she'd come to the class to practise, not to learn. I could see that most of the other people didn't like her much. As I came nearer to her this woman turned round. And she looked me up and down and said, "Oh dear, please tell me he's here to fix the central heating. Because there is no way I'm dancing with *that*."'

'What a nightmare! What did you say?'

'Nothing. I turned around and left and I never went back.'

'What a shame. I can't believe anyone else thought like she did. She sounds awful.'

'Maybe, but they'd heard what she thought of me,' Mick said. 'And once it was in their heads, how would I get it out? I'd always be the man who should be fixing the central heating. I'd always be the man who was "*that*".'

Mick was right. The problem wasn't everyone else agreeing with the person who called you names. The problem was that once they were said out loud, the names were in everyone's head.

If there are people in need, Giant will find them . . .

No one is too small for Giant to hear.

Giant sees and hears everyone . . .

But is there anyone to hear Giant?

Elise's Plan

I should have known Elise wouldn't stand for silence for long. Elise doesn't stand anything she doesn't like for long. She caught me at the end of lunch when I was just finishing off the trees for the forest in *Snow White*. The leaves were really fiddly to do.

'What do you think you're doing, Anzo?' Elise was standing with her arms folded across her chest and she was glaring at me.

'I'm finishing off the forest. Ms Brown likes me doing the trees because I can reach. That's funny, isn't it, when you think how I wouldn't have been able to do this last year.' I was babbling, but that was the nerves. Elise is the kind of person you don't want mad at you. And she was definitely mad.

'Why are you avoiding me?'

'I'm not avoiding you. I'm painting trees,' I told her.

Elise narrowed her eyes at me. When Elise narrows her eyes her whole face seems to go narrow as well. 'You're painting trees to avoid me.'

This was true, but I wasn't going to admit it.

'I'm painting trees to help Ms Brown.'

Elise didn't say anything for a minute. She just stood, her arms still folded, tapping her right foot. 'Anzo, what's going on? Did I say something to make you angry?'

I took my brush and filled in another leaf on the tree very, very carefully. 'No, of course not.'

She took a step closer. 'Is it something to do with your family?'

I squinted at the leaf and put a bit more paint on even though it didn't need any. 'No.' The 'no' didn't sound very convincing. And if it didn't sound very convincing to me, it was definitely not going to sound convincing to Elise.

'Anzo . . .'

Sometimes Elise's silences were stronger than her words. She just looked at me.

There's really no point arguing with Elise.

'Come to my house after school,' she said. It wasn't an invitation; it was an order.

* * *

When I'd finished telling her about my family's having said no about going to Comic Con, Elise sat on her bed, hugging her knees to her chest like she always did when she was thinking. I liked being in Elise's house. It was always tidy and had a fresh, clean smell. It was a calm house too. It felt like the sort of place where people had proper conversations in quiet voices. Not big, loud shouting ones where no one could hear you.

After a while she sat up straight and swung her legs onto the floor. 'You'll need to bring that mini camcorder you got last Christmas so you can video Jesse Edward's talk. You won't take all of it in the first time, you know. Concentration levels can go down when you're excited.'

'I just told you, I'm *not* going.'

'Yes, you are.'

I looked at her. 'Right. And I bet you already have a plan.'

'Of *course* I already have a plan.'

Elise had her 'Facing Down a Gale Force Wind'

look. It was a look I knew not to mess with. One time when we were about seven, we had an argument about whether Father Christmas's reindeer slept in his house or had their own stable. Elise was sure they shared his house and I thought they'd have a stable because they were more like horses than people. Elise had about a million reasons to prove me wrong, starting with Rudolph's nose and ending with their ability to fly (I had to admit I'd never seen a horse that could do that). I hadn't stood a chance.

I'd learned a lot from that argument. Mainly, don't argue with Elise.

I changed my approach. '*How* am I going if my mum and dad have said no and I don't have the money?' All my savings were in a bank account that I needed my parents' permission to get out, and I knew that my piggy bank didn't have anywhere near the amount that the trip to the Comic Con would cost. 'And it's not like I can just turn up on my own.'

Elise sighed as if I was being exceptionally slow. 'You won't be going on your own, will you? *I'll* go with you.'

'But you're not a grown-up. They'll expect me to have a grown-up with me.'

'*You'll* be the grown-up. You'll be my older brother, taking me there.'

'Oh, why didn't you say so?' I said. 'It'll be a piece of cake then.'

Elise's sarcasm detector was apparently turned off. 'Yes.'

'No, it *won't* be.'

She tilted her chin up at me. 'This is your thing, Anzo. This is how you'll get people to pay attention to you in the future.'

By 'people', Elise meant my family.

'And just because they don't take what you love to do seriously, it doesn't mean you don't have to.'

'What about the money?' I didn't know how to argue with her other points so I decided to stick with asking questions. 'There's the train tickets, and the food and the accommodation at the hotel.'

'I've been saving up Christmas and birthday money for the last five years. I have enough for the travel and the tickets, especially with your discount.' Elise picked up a hairband and pulled her hair back into a neat little ponytail, letting the band snap into place. Elise was a very *efficient* person. 'I can cover it.'

'You've been saving up to go to the

International Cartoon Strip Association Comic Con for *five years?*'

'No, you idiot. I've just been saving up for something big. And this is it.'

That's the thing about Elise. She might go on about psychology and be a bit bossy (OK, *very* bossy) and have a tendency to think she's always right. She might sound like a walking wind chime and never let you keep things to yourself. But she was a really, really good friend.

* * *

That night Night Owl Bob was interviewing truck drivers. One guy called Steve who phoned in did night shifts. He started work around four o'clock in the afternoon and finished around six in the morning. Bob asked him what it felt like to drive at night.

'You get in this trance,' Steve said. 'You're watching the lines in the road, because really they're the only thing that you can always see ahead of you. Sometimes I don't even remember the roads I took to get somewhere because all I was paying attention to was the lines and the thoughts in my head.' He was quiet for a second. 'It's funny – even though it's dark and you can't see much, so many things are clearer at night than they are in the day.' Steve was right. Sometimes it took thinking about things at night to see them clearly. I knew now I needed something more than growing taller to solve my problems. I just didn't know if travelling two hundred and fifty miles to see Jesse Edward and a bunch of cartoons was the answer.

Discovering a
Superpower

Mum had finished the restaurant dining room and the kitchen and had started work on the toilets. Uncle Miles had begun to cook ten different dishes a day in his quest to finalise the menu. Dad and Uncle Talbert had taken over Mum's wallpaper table and were using it as their centre of operations for all the forms that needed filling in. As they got closer and closer to being able to open the restaurant, they all developed the same kind of line that Miss Bentley had had in the middle of her forehead when I was still all seven dwarfs in *Snow White*.

I walked into the kitchen after school one afternoon, put my bag down and went to get a glass of milk from the enormous industrial-sized fridge. Usually someone in the family would give me a 'Hey, Anzo', but in the last few weeks they'd stopped even looking up from what they were doing. Mum was drilling something somewhere upstairs, Uncle Miles was cooking at the new stove and Dad and Uncle Talbert were at their 'desk' at the back, deep in conversation.

'The trouble is, we can't advertise until we have a name,' Dad was saying. 'I've started researching people to design the menus and the posters, but we can't commit to a style until we have a name to design around.' He had a pile of sample drawings and logos in front of him. 'It's hard enough knowing how to make a decision about the look as it is.'

I came a bit closer and picked one up – I could see how the designer understood colour and had what Ms Brown called 'a tight grip on composition'. This was the first bit of the restaurant business I could help with, the first part of it that was about something I understood. I opened my mouth to tell Dad about Ms Brown's way of deciding whether a design worked when he noticed what I was holding.

'Oh, Anzo, please don't muck about with the

designs, I've only just got them in order. Can you just give us some room to talk about this in peace?'

I dropped the design on the desk and picked up my bag, backing away towards the door.

Uncle Miles plonked a dish of deep-fried butternut squash and chilli dumplings in front of Dad and Uncle Talbert. 'Taste these. All we need is a bit of inspiration – and *that's* what my food does. Remember, we're trying to replace the bland suffocation of our childhoods with something a bit more exciting in our adult lives.'

'I hope you're not suggesting we call the restaurant "Inspiration",' Uncle Talbert said. 'We want people to digest their food, not feel like throwing up.'

They hadn't noticed me come in and they didn't notice me leave either. I'd given Giant the superpowers of height and strength. But it turned out I had a superpower of my own: invisibility.

*   *   *

Night Owl Bob had so many callers to his programme on loneliness that he decided to do another one on the same subject. I wondered if anyone else listened to Bob to get his advice about stuff. I don't think that was what his show was meant for really. But it was only after I heard a woman called Gina call in that I knew that going to the Comic Con with Elise was what I really wanted to do.

'People think loneliness is about being on your own,' she told Bob, 'but it isn't; it's about not connecting. Do you know what I mean?'

'I think I do,' Bob told her.

Gina didn't seem to hear him, she was too caught up in what she was saying. 'It's like, you could be at a huge party, every room filled with people, but you could still feel as if you were standing in the middle of a field or a desert with no other person for miles and miles. And actually, you feel worse, because all the people around you are reminding you of how unconnected you are, because they're all laughing and chatting away, they're all perfectly happy.'

'What about social media – Facebook, Twitter? Don't you find them good ways of connecting with people?'

'I hate Facebook! I hate all that stupid social media!' Gina said it so loudly you could imagine Bob flinching. 'It's evil! Endless photos of people on holiday, or with their friends or boyfriends or girlfriends, showing off about how happy and successful they are, how their lives are *completely perfect*. I don't find that helpful. I find that *unhelpful*.'

'Their lives might not be as perfect as they seem,' Bob pointed out.

'Yeah, well,' Gina said. 'It doesn't matter, because all of it just reminds me that I don't have anyone to talk to. My friends have all moved away, my mum left years ago and my dad's at work all the time.' She paused. 'And even when I'm with people these days, I feel like I'm on my own.'

I heard laughing from downstairs. Uncle Talbert had announced at dinner that he was going to prove once and for all that he was the master of accents out of the three brothers. Dad had tried to protest and so had Uncle Miles, but Uncle Talbert had turned it into a competition and that made it irresistible. I'd thought about telling them about the accents Ms Bentley had tried to teach me, but since none of them had stuck, there hadn't seemed much point. I didn't know how to make the story funny. I didn't know how to make them laugh. I didn't know how to be 'big' the way they were big – doing everything as if they were live onstage. What it boiled down to was that I didn't know how to be extraordinary like them. Every day I was growing taller, but when I was around my family I felt smaller than ever. I knew what Gina meant. Even when I was with them, I felt like I was on my own.

Putting the Plan into Action

As plans go, Elise's was pretty solid. This wasn't surprising because, as you already know, Elise is a very organised person.

The International Cartoon Strip Association Comic Con was on a weekend, starting on Friday night and ending Sunday afternoon, so we didn't have to worry about school. I was supposed to tell my parents that I was staying at Elise's, and Elise would say she was staying at mine. Elise had worked out that if we left as soon as the Comic Con finished, we'd be back home at about the time our parents would be expecting us. Mine might not notice if I disappeared for a bit, but hers definitely would.

Even by her family's usual high organisational

standards, Elise had had a field day with her Post-it preparations. She'd planned out everything from the first mention of our planned weekend visit ('Tell them on Thursday – that way it's too late for them to object, but not so late that they get suspicious'), to the train times ('We'll take the 15.53 going up Friday afternoon, then get the 14.54 coming back on Sunday, just in time for dinner at home'). We'd have our phones with us so we could easily send them messages if they did ask questions ('I'll send some convincing updates every now and then just to keep them quiet'). She'd registered me as an adult on the International Cartoon Strip Association convention website ('Though we'll say you're just eighteen – the height's convincing enough but I'm not sure your personality is') and herself as my little sister ('They'll think it's sweet of you to take me').

It felt like I'd jumped on a train as it left the station and then realised I didn't know if it was going in the right direction. But any time I started to express any doubts, Elise would give me her 'Facing Down a Gale Force Wind' look. And that would be that.

* * *

Making sure I got a 'yes' from my parents about going to Elise's house for the weekend was all about timing and confidence. I needed to ask Mum when she was doing some DIY, because she hated stopping work once she'd started. And I needed to be confident that she'd say yes (Chapter Three of *The Power of Positive Thinking* – 'expecting agreement is the path to getting agreement'). The timing bit was fairly easy. Mum was so focused on getting the decorating finished that she barely did anything else these days. Uncle Miles couldn't get her to sit down to meals any more so he was making her endless plates of finger food. There were little side dishes on every surface with half-eaten nibbles. And the dining room had become a kind of no-go zone, with Mum or Dad or Uncle Miles or Uncle Talbert yelling, 'WET PAINT!' whenever you went in.

I told my mum that I was staying at Elise's while she was doing a particularly tricky bit of the ceiling. She pushed back the scarf she was wearing to protect her hair from the paint. 'Um, you mean for the whole weekend? Won't Elise's parents mind?'

'We're working on a special school project and want to spend a lot of time on it this weekend. Elise's parents said it would be a pleasure to have me.'

('Elise's parents said it would be a pleasure to have me,' had been on a blue Post-it note.)

Mum noticed a drip of paint above her head and quickly reached up to smooth it out with the tip of her brush. You could see her mind was already moving on to the next patch of ceiling that needed her attention. 'Well then, all right. Don't be any trouble to them, will you?'

'I won't.' I watched for a second as she carried on painting, thinking she might ask a question. But she didn't, so I went upstairs to pack my bag. It occurred to me that I could have gone a lot further than two hundred and fifty miles away without them noticing.

Unknowables

The difference between having a plan and carrying out a plan is that when you just have a plan, in your head or on paper, everything goes smoothly. You know, exactly as you planned. But when you actually come to carry out the plan, what happens is that all the unexpected things that you couldn't possibly have known about or planned for come up and change it. Then what you have is a plan plus *unknowables*.

Unknowables are not something you want to have as part of your plan.

At first everything went according to the Post-its. We met at the corner of my road with our bags and caught the bus to the station. The only tricky bit was when we got on the bus and the driver didn't believe I should have a child fare.

'There's no way you're under twelve,' he told me.

'I'm just tall for my age.'

The bus driver laughed nastily. His laugh sounded a bit like Josh's. I wondered if they were related.

I was about to protest when Elise jabbed me in the side and hissed, 'May as well start your cover now.'

'What?'

'You're my *older* brother,' she whispered.

'Oh, right.' I turned back to the bus driver. 'Actually, I'll take an adult ticket.'

'Oh, you will, will you? That's good of you.' The driver leaned forward to get a laugh from the other people nearby. He and Josh were *definitely* from the same gene pool. I laughed too as if it was all a joke, because what else could I do? He was the driver; I couldn't annoy him or else we'd get thrown off the bus. That's the thing about people with power – they can't help showing off that they've got it.

We got our tickets, moved to the back of the bus and sat down. I looked around and realised that being a grown-up really just meant *pretending* you were grown up. If you were tall enough, if you looked the part, people would believe you.

That wasn't the only thing being tall meant. Ever since I'd become as tall as some of the teachers at school, they seemed to expect me to behave like them. It was as if every inch I'd grown added a year to my age. I knew not everything in my life was about height, but I couldn't help thinking that appearances made a lot more difference than they should.

*   *   *

At the train station Elise didn't act like a little sister. She acted like a mum. A really strict one.

'You can't buy a slushie,' she told me, sounding shocked, when I stopped in front of the slushie bar. 'You can get a coffee or something instead.'

'But I don't like coffee!'

'Well, grown-ups don't drink slushies so you can't have one.'

'How do you know?'

'Have you *ever* seen a grown-up with a blue slushie tongue?'

Elise is very good at coming up with questions I can't answer. In the end she let me buy a bottle of water and a packet of crisps. (Of course *she* was allowed a slushie.)

* * *

On the train, Elise reread *The Power of Positive Thinking* in case she'd missed anything. I didn't know quite what she was expecting to find, unless there was a chapter on impersonating grown-ups and successfully lying to your family.

So basically everything was going well. Until the train stopped in the middle of nowhere.

There was no sign of a station outside the window. The only thing in sight was a house with a garden that backed onto the tracks. The low fence had collapsed, showing a tatty trampoline and a yellow ride-on truck designed for toddlers. The trampoline reminded me of something Uncle Talbert had said the other night.

'Remember, Anzo, when you get really tall, it's impossible to bounce on beds without coming a cropper. So bounce while you can. Once you get to a certain height, all your childish games are over.' He'd sighed and clutched his chest in his usual dramatic fashion and Uncle Miles had laughed.

'You've never stopped being a kid, you fool,' Uncle Miles had told Uncle Talbert.

Uncle Talbert patted me on the shoulder. 'Well, remember this one still is – and should be allowed to be – not like—'

Then a timer went off in the kitchen and Uncle Miles dragged Uncle Talbert away to help him peel carrots for dinner.

* * *

After ten minutes the train still hadn't moved. All we'd heard from the announcer was something garbled about 'regretting any inconvenience for this short but necessary stop to ensure your ongoing safety'. Elise was usually a calm sort of person, but even she was getting jittery.

'We need to get there so we can register before the introductory session.' She pressed her nose to the glass of the window, as if the extra pressure might make the train move. 'They might say something about the competition, something you need to know.'

'Don't worry, sis.' I thought it was a good opportunity to practise my cover as the mature older brother.

'You don't have to talk like that *now*.' Elise's bracelets jangled as she shifted grumpily in her seat.

The tannoy crackled into life. 'We apologise for the delay, ladies and gentleman,' said a man with a whiny voice (or maybe that was the effect of the tannoy). 'Regrettably this service will be forced to terminate at this junction. A replacement service will be along very shortly. This action is being taken for your safety and convenience.'

'Convenience!' a man behind us said loudly. 'What's convenient about being kicked off a train in the middle of nowhere?'

'And how long is it going to take?' Elise looked right at me, as if I would know the answer. Was my height even making *her* think I was older?

'I'm sure it won't take long,' I told her. It felt like an older-brother thing to say and weirdly it worked. Elise settled back into her seat and stopped looking so panicked.

After the announcement had been made the ticket inspector came through the carriage. As soon as he appeared, people started yelling out questions – asking where we were, and how long it was going to take before we got a new train, and was it going to be a train or a coach (one woman was particularly concerned about the toilet facilities) and whether there would be refunds and free refreshments to make up for the delay. I couldn't help feeling sorry for him as he tried to answer all the questions at once, especially as it was obvious that he didn't know the answers to most of them. Then his walkie-talkie bleeped and he listened to it for a moment or two. At first he looked a bit worried, and then he looked over in our direction. As soon as he spotted me he looked relieved. Now all the worry that *he'd* been feeling was transferred to me.

He walked over, pushing his way past the man who'd been concerned about the free sandwiches, and stopped in front of our table seat.

'Excuse me, sir?'

It took a second for me to realise that he really was talking to me. I wasn't a grown-up, I was in a Year 6 class! I was a frog, not a 'sir'! Luckily Elise kicked me under the table before I said anything that might give me away.

The ticket inspector didn't seem to notice my expression of pure terror and kept talking. 'I'm wondering if you could lend some assistance,' he said. 'You see, I need to clear all the carriages on this train as quickly as possible so that we can get this defective train off the line, ready for the replacement train which will be arriving shortly.'

'Um, OK.' When you don't have a clue what's going on it's generally best to keep your comments to a minimum.

'The problem is that I've been instructed to make sure customers are gathered in one place – health and safety, you understand,' the ticket inspector went on.

I kept looking at him. Was I supposed to mind-read what he wanted?

'As we're not at an actual station.'

'I see.' I didn't.

'The thing is –' the ticket inspector ploughed on in a what-the-hell kind of way – 'given you're so, uh, tall, I thought you might be willing to lend a hand.'

'You mean . . .' I had no idea what he meant, but usually if you start a sentence, grown-ups will jump in and finish it for you.

'You could be our meeting point,' he said. He smiled at me in what he probably thought was a winning fashion.

'So what you're saying is, you want my brother to be a beacon,' Elise said.

'Well, not exactly a *beacon*,' the ticket inspector said, his neck starting to flush under his navy-blue uniform.

Elise nodded. 'Yes, *exactly* like a beacon.' She turned to me. 'You don't mind, do you, Anzo?'

It's funny how tone is a lot more important than words. Because yet again there wasn't a question mark on the end of Elise's question. She was *telling* me that I didn't mind.

I didn't much like the idea of being a human beacon, but Elise hadn't given me any choice. I'm not sure what I could have said anyway – that I was phobic about standing at the centre of large crowds?

'You don't want me to make a speech or anything, do you?' Just the thought of the possibility made my throat tighten.

'Oh no, no, no,' the ticket inspector said. 'Like the little girl said, just be a beacon.' He laughed. 'It's really handy you're here, sir. You're made for the job.'

'OK then,' I said. 'Um, where do you want me to go?'

The ticket inspector, who introduced himself as Dave, and got very chatty once I'd agreed to help, led us through all the other passengers, whose complaints and questions had settled down into a muttering grumble, and outside the train.

'Thanks so much for helping out, mate,' Dave said.

At least agreeing to help had stopped him from calling me sir. (I'd decided I never wanted to be called sir again, even when I *was* older – it was too weird.)

'Would you believe it, this is the first time I've done this route.' Dave was getting ready to talk into his walkie-talkie, but that didn't seem to stop him from talking to me. 'And look what goes and happens! One hundred and seventy-two grumpy customers moaning on about free sandwiches is what happens.' He paused to mumble something into his walkie-talkie and then turned back to me. 'You wouldn't believe what the general public can be like, you really wouldn't.'

'Apart from us,' Elise told Dave.

'Exactly,' Dave said. 'It's helpful people like you that keep me going, let me tell you.' He turned and squinted up the track. 'Now, sir, if I could ask you to hold your arm up for a minute or two, just until the word's gone round that you're the meeting point, that would be fantastic.'

I stuck my hand up in the air. Dave blew on

his whistle so sharply I thought I'd done something wrong and brought it down again.

'No, no, keep your hand up, that's it.' Then he rushed back into the carriage.

For a second I thought that it was all some plot to abandon us by the tracks, but then I realised he'd just gone back inside to tell people to come out. As soon as all the passengers saw me there was a kind of a stampede. Elise had to stand in front of me to stop people from actually pushing me over. I was less like a human beacon and more like a human skittle.

Dave was right, I didn't have to make a speech. But I still spent the next forty-five minutes telling one hundred and seventy-two people that I didn't know if they'd be getting any free sandwiches.

Facing the Nightmare

By the time we arrived at the hotel we were exactly an hour behind schedule. Maybe that's what led to the next unknowable happening. Or maybe it was that my experience of being a human beacon made me look more like a point of contact.

As we walked into the foyer, a woman sitting by the door holding a clipboard got up to greet us. She picked up the large holdall by her feet and slung it over one shoulder as she came up to us. 'Oh, good, you've arrived.'

I guess Elise and I both assumed that this was part of the standard welcome for the convention so we just smiled. 'Sorry we're late,' I said. I pushed my shoulders back and tried to look as grown-up as possible. I stopped smiling and put on a little frown. Grown-ups wear little frowns a lot. (I think what they're trying to get across is an impression that they're terribly busy and much too important to muck about, but really all they look is grumpy.) I felt pretty confident at this point. After my meeting-point experience, I thought I'd got the hang of this whole acting-like-an-adult thing.

The woman seemed to be distracted as she rootled around in the bag. 'Hmm? Oh, that's all right. You know what the start of these things is always like, with over-excited attendees running everywhere.'

'We've not been before actually.'

'We? Oh, is this . . . ?'

'My little sister. Elise. It was a surprise for her.'

The woman looked at us properly for the first time. Her eyebrows went up into little triangles. 'I see. For me too. I didn't realise we'd OK'd that.'

Elise and I exchanged a glance – was there some rule about kids coming that we hadn't seen? And if so, what if they found out that we were *both* kids?

The woman sighed. 'Oh well, I don't suppose it matters. Frankly we're too hard pressed to worry about anything except getting this talk done.'

'So we haven't missed the introductory talk?' Elise smiled with relief.

The woman laughed. 'Well, that would be hard, wouldn't it, given it's your brother who's giving it?'

It took a second for her words to sink in.

Unfortunately that was exactly a second too long to explain the mistake.

One thing I was learning was that when adults get what they want, they can move *really* fast.

The next thing we knew, the woman had thrust the bag at me, then taken a sheet from the clipboard and laid it on top of the bag.

'The whole thing shouldn't take more than five minutes,' she said. 'Just run through all the items on the list, give everyone a badge and tell them to grab a tea or coffee before the first talk.' She pointed to a pair of double doors off the reception hall. 'Everything's set up for you on the stage through there. Sorry there isn't time to do a sound check but, well, you were late!' She patted Elise on the shoulder. 'You can help your big brother by being nice and quiet, can't you?' Before Elise could say what was on the tip of her tongue (and I could see that it wasn't going to be nice or quiet), the woman had turned and run off towards the lifts, calling out behind her, 'We'll give you five minutes before we send everyone in. See you later!' We watched as she slipped into the lift and the doors closed after her.

I looked at the sheet. It had big bold capitals across the top:

HEALTH AND SAFETY GUIDELINES FOR ATTENDEES OF THE INTERNATIONAL CARTOON STRIP ASSOCIATION COMIC CON

Then there was a list underneath of things like where the fire exits were. Elise grabbed the list before I'd read past the first couple of lines. My skin was officially on fire. There was absolutely no way I could do this.

Elise put her hand on my arm. 'Anzo, relax. It's no big deal.' She stuck her hand in the bag and pulled out a badge that had a cartoon elf on it holding a placard that said, 'The International Cartoon Strip Association Comic Con believes in "elf" and safety!'

'There's absolutely no way I can do this,' I said, this time out loud.

Elise pretended I hadn't spoken and started gently pulling me by the arm towards the big double doors. They looked huge. Probably because they were the entrance to my nightmare. 'She must have thought you were one of the helpers. All you have to do is read this out to everyone and then give them a badge.'

'I mean it. I really can't do this.'

She was pulling us closer to the Nightmare Doors now, still ignoring me. 'Hey, maybe you'll get some sort of prize or special treatment for doing this.'

'What for – impersonating one of the organisers?' What was she *saying*? It was as if Elise had forgotten who I was.

'Helpers, not organisers. And you're not impersonating – it's just a case of mistaken identity.'

'Whatever it is, I'm not doing it.'

'You have to – you're on in five minutes.'

'Elise, how many people are coming to this weekend?'

Elise shrugged. 'I don't know – two hundred? Three hundred?'

'I am *not* standing up in front of three hundred people and telling them where the fire exits are and handing out stupid badges. You know I can't do it.'

'You won't have to hand the badges out – we can put them in bowls at the door.'

'Elise.'

Elise stopped walking and looked up at me. 'Anzo, this is why we came here this weekend.'

'So that I could become a health and safety expert and hand out the unfunniest badges ever made?'

'To prove yourself. To show what you're capable of.'

'To a bunch of strangers?'

Elise poked me in the chest with her forefinger. Her bangles jangled. 'No, we came here to prove to *you* what you're capable of, Anzo. Because if you get it, everyone else will get it too. That's what confidence is. It's the difference between "So what?" and "That's brilliant." Confidence is the kind of magic that makes you believe in yourself – so that the whole world sees you as amazing as you are.'

'*The Power of Positive Thinking*?'

Elise sniffed. 'I am capable of a rousing speech myself, you know.'

I waited.

'Chapter six,' she admitted. 'But it's all true!'

134

I looked at the doors.

'Anzo. You can do this. You're my big brother. You can do anything. Come on.' Elise took the bag from me, slung it over her shoulder and headed through the double doors.

What did I do? I followed her, that's what I did.

* * *

Night Owl Bob did a show about fear once. People phoned in all night to talk about the things they were most scared of. There was fear of all the usual things of course – spiders, heights, water, ghosts, clowns – and then there were the odder ones – the colour yellow, cheese, dinner parties, knees. What they all described was what I felt over the next five minutes: a hammering heart, the back of my neck prickling with sweat, my legs feeling heavy and numb. The difference between all those callers and me was that they all kept away from their fears. I was stupid enough to be running straight towards mine.

* * *

The stage looked to be a million miles wide. In the middle of it was a microphone and a stand, where Elise said I needed to be. In front of the stage were seventy billion chairs. Roughly. Elise dumped the badges on the tables near the doors and then came up to stand beside me with the sheet of paper.

'All you have to do is read this,' she said. 'They won't be expecting you to be entertaining or anything. In fact, they'll be expecting you to be incredibly boring, so that makes it even easier.'

'I'm not worried about being entertaining. I'm worried about passing out.'

'Look, you were being a human beacon to hundreds of train passengers an hour ago. What's the difference?'

'I didn't have to talk to the train passengers. That's the difference.'

'Yes, you did. You kept telling them you didn't know if there would be any free sandwiches.'

'But I wasn't *expected* to talk. I was just talking because people were talking to me. There's a huge difference!'

'Anzo,' Elise said, looking up into my eyes, 'if you can talk to a large hall of strangers then you won't be frightened of talking to your family.'

'I'm not *frightened* of talking to them!'

Elise looked at me.

'I'm not! I'm just—'

'Terrified of saying the wrong thing? Scared of boring them?'

'Maybe.'

'And that's why they don't know how much you love drawing cartoons!'

I looked down at the sheet of instructions I was supposed to read out. I needed to get familiar with them if I was going to have any hope of not messing this up.

'Anzo?'

'Yes.'

'This is exactly what you need. Believe me, it's the start of your journey to happiness.'

I was about to tell her that it was the start of my journey to major humiliation, but Elise had that look on her face. The look that said I may as well get ready to talk to a roomful of strangers because there was no way I was going to get out of it. There was a gale-force wind coming.

* * *

When the first people came in I felt my throat tighten and I couldn't remember how to breathe. Elise pushed me towards the microphone and whispered, 'Good luck.'

As more and more people filed in I went into a kind of trance. In a way it was better onstage. I couldn't really see all the people because of the way the lights were angled. I could just hear lots of chattering, laughing and shuffling of feet. I told myself that they weren't all whispering and laughing about me and hoped I was right. I looked down at the sheet of paper. The paper was shaking.

There was a clock on the wall, but the second hand seemed to have gone into slow motion. It was like being in a sci-fi film at the moment of disaster. Elise came up to the foot of the stage and whispered that all the seats were taken. I took a breath.

'Helloeveryone, thisisthelistofallthehealthand safetythingsyouneedtoknow.'

Elise appeared at the foot of the stage again. She waved. I gave her a 'Why Did You Make Me Do This' look.

'S-l-o-w . . . *d-o-w-n*,' she mouthed.

I nodded. 'Number . . . one . . . In . . . case . . . of . . . fire . . .'

Someone giggled.

I looked up. I stared out at the sea of people. Most of them were *professional cartoonists*. They were the people I wanted to grow up to be

like. An image of Dad came into my mind –
standing at the head of the table, holding his
arms out as if welcoming everyone into them,
a big smile on his face, knowing that everyone
would listen to him.

Confidence is a kind of magic.

I decided to give *The Power of Positive Thinking*
a go.

I gave Elise a nod, took a breath, and lifted
up my head and smiled. I tried again. It wasn't
perfect and I think I sped up again, but at least
I kept smiling.

Maybe I wasn't like Dad, but that didn't mean
I had to be completely *unlike* him either.

* * *

Afterwards, when I came down off the stage, I
realised I'd forgotten to say anything about the
badges, but Elise said it didn't matter; everyone
seemed to know to take one anyway.

I stood beaming at everyone as they passed
by. The woman who'd given me the bag and
the paper came up to us. She was looking at
me the way someone might look at a pepperoni
and mushroom pizza when they'd actually
ordered a margherita. 'Well, that was . . .

interesting. How long exactly have you been working for the temp agency?'

'We're not from an agency. We just booked to come here.'

'You mean you're ordinary attendees?'

'Yes.'

'Your name isn't –' she checked her list – 'Elijah Ferrall-Tyler?'

I shook my head.

The woman kept staring at me intently. I wasn't just a pepperoni and mushroom, I was the *oddest* pepperoni and mushroom pizza she'd ever seen – pepperoni and mushroom with chocolate chips. 'But . . . why didn't you just say so?'

'My brother likes to be helpful,' Elise told the woman. 'He's extremely mature for his age.'

'I see,' the woman said, in that tone of voice that adults use when they mean the opposite of what they're actually saying. 'Well, it doesn't matter, I suppose – and since the other chap hasn't appeared to turn up it's a good thing you stepped in.' She gave us a small smile. 'So thank you – that was certainly the . . . *most interesting* presentation we've ever had.'

'Shall we go and check in now?'

Elise took my arm. 'Yes, let's do that.' She

turned to the woman. 'I hope you'll remember how helpful Anzo was.'

The woman's eyebrows shot up into those little triangles again, but she nodded. 'Yes, I'll remember.'

As soon as we were outside the hall, Elise pulled me to one side. 'You'll be feeling tired now.'

As soon as she said it, I felt exhaustion flood through me.

'Is your mouth dry?'

'Wait – am I ill or something?' It was a bit freaky having someone tell you things you felt and then feeling them right away.

'No, but when you're been in a state of nervous excitement your body produces loads of adrenaline. Then after it leaves the body you feel a bit rubbish.'

With all the stuff she knows from her mum and dad, and even with her wanting to be a therapist, Elise is basically a GP in training. That's not as good as it sounds, because sometimes she knows enough to tell someone they're really not well but she can't tell them what to do to feel better. In this case though, apparently all I had to do was sit down and have a cup of tea.

It was the first thing I'd done that day that wasn't difficult.

A New Friend

The whole hotel had been taken over by the Comic Con. Everywhere we went were exhibit boards covered with original Marvel cartoons, photos and bios of the guest speakers, notices about comic critique groups, clubs and competitions. People stood in small groups, discussing different comic-book styles or comparing recent buys. There was an area devoted to stalls for artists to display and sell their original work and another dedicated to selling stuff like T-shirts, mugs and pens.

'I can just see Giant on a T-shirt,' Elise said, pointing at a T-shirt with the Incredible Hulk bursting out of his shirt. Across the bottom of the hulk's legs the T-shirt read: 'You wouldn't like me when I'm angry.'

'Yeah. An extra-large one.' For a second I let myself imagine being one of the artists standing behind their stalls, talking to admirers of their work. At home I was surrounded by people who did what they loved every day. Now I knew what it felt like.

On our way to the first workshop session, Elise stopped by a large poster about the Comic Con cartoon competition.

She turned to me. 'You brought all your Giant strips, right?'

'Yeah.' It had been advised on the website that all attendees should bring samples of their work, so they could get feedback in workshops or just so they could share them with other artists. I wasn't quite up to thinking of myself as an artist yet, but I'd brought them anyway.

'Including the new one?'

'Yeah. Why?

Elise nodded at the poster. 'Because I think you should enter the competition.'

I stared up at the poster. Somehow the thought of entering the competition here made me nervous.

'I can't.'

'Why not? You entered the other one.'

'That was different – that had different age categories.'

Elise leaned forward and scanned the list of rules. 'So what? This one's for all ages – that includes you.'

'But look who's come to this – they're nearly all proper comic-book artists.'

'Like you,' Elise said.

'No, not like me.'

'Anzo, look around you,' Elise said. 'You're one of them.'

I looked around me. I'd expected to get stared at a lot at the convention since that's what had happened ever since I'd grown past 'normal' height, but no one here seemed to notice. I was surrounded by people who loved reading the same things, doing the same things.

Maybe Elise was right. Maybe I *was* one of them.

* * *

The sessions we went to that evening were so good that I couldn't really talk afterwards. Picture the thing you love doing most in the world. Now picture a roomful of people who all love that same thing just as much as you do – and

144

not only do they love it, they know so much about it that you want to download everything they know into your head.

There was a session on the history of comic strips, and one on adventure strips and one on drawing techniques. It was like going into a sweet shop and being told you could have anything. It was lucky that Elise's Post-it note organising had included a reminder to bring several notebooks, because by the end of Friday night my first one was almost full. And we hadn't even had the talk from Jesse Edward yet!

Just before dinner, I got into conversation with a man called Eric. He had curly hair that stuck out in all directions and wore a green velvet coat that reached down to his knees. He had a pen behind each ear and a row of five in his coat pocket. When he saw me noticing, he grinned at me and opened up his coat – two huge pockets each held an A4 drawing pad. 'Be prepared, my friend, be prepared.'

'So you have ideas all the time?'

He shrugged, smiling. 'Not necessarily good ones. But it's getting them down that's important. Like in improv, say "yes" to everything.'

'Improv?'

'Improvisation. You know, when people get

onstage and make up a scene on the spot using audience suggestions. The rule is that you say yes to whatever people suggest or whatever comes into your head.'

'Doesn't that go wrong sometimes?'

Eric laughed. '*Oh* yeah.'

It had been bad enough standing up onstage with a piece of paper telling me what to say. I couldn't imagine getting up in front of an audience *not* knowing what to say. I shuddered and Eric laughed again.

'That's the thing, my friend – if you want to get better at something, you have to face the scary, don't you?'

I thought about the health and safety talk and how I still felt really happy about it. Not because I'd been good at it (I knew I hadn't) but just because I'd done it. And the next time I faced the scary, maybe it might actually go well. 'Yeah, I guess you do.'

* * *

Dinner was a buffet held in the same hall where I'd given the health and safety talk. I'd had a couple of people recognise me but they'd been really nice about it (meaning no one laughed at me). When Elise and I queued up for our plates of food I tried to say a few big-brother things like, 'Don't forget to get some broccoli,' but Elise gave me a death stare so I shut up. We found a table near the door, where we could leave quickly if we got asked any awkward questions. Everyone around us was laughing a lot as they drank wine and beer, and I suddenly felt that pretending to be a grown-up when you were actually only nearly twelve wasn't as easy as Elise had made out. A woman a few seats away was telling a funny story about something that had happened at another Comic Con and she kept putting on different accents for the different people in it. She did a Scottish accent and a French accent and then a Swedish accent. She wasn't as bad as I'd been when I was the seven dwarfs, but she didn't do any of them as well as my dad and Uncle Talbert and Uncle Miles could.

I wondered if the ticket inspector was on the train on its way back. Even though I loved nearly everything about the Comic Con, a part of me wouldn't have minded being on that train now, heading home. It would have been nice to hear Uncle Talbert making fun of Uncle Miles's latest dinner creation. It would even have been nice to hear Mum drilling somewhere in the house as Dad sang at Volume 11 over the restaurant paperwork. I wondered if they had thought about me since I left, and then realised how stupid that was – they were way too busy with the restaurant to even notice I'd gone.

* * *

After dinner we worked until about eleven o'clock redrafting my comic-strip entry. Elise had seen some samples of other people's work and it had made her more determined to make mine perfect. I must have redrawn the last panels five times before she was satisfied. At last she nodded. 'OK, it's done.'

'Good, because my fingers are about to fall off.'

'You won't be complaining when you're using them to get a well-done handshake. And when you go home and show your mum and dad the trophy.'

'How do you know there's a trophy?' I wished she hadn't mentioned it, because it made me want to win. Mum and Dad could ignore an Honourable Mention, but could they ignore a trophy?

'Saw it.' Elise was one of those people who knew *everything*.

I thought of all those people in the hall, all those professional cartoonists. 'I don't think I'm going to win, Elise. Everyone here is a proper cartoonist.'

'So are you.'

'How do you know?'

'Because you draw all the time. You draw when you're happy, when you're sad, when you've been cast as all seven dwarfs in the school play. It's who you are.'

'But what if I *don't* win.' I was starting to worry that Elise would feel really let down if I didn't. Five years of Christmas and birthday money makes for a lot of pressure. If you think about it, what she was expecting was one *ginormous* present. And I wasn't sure I could supply it.

Elise raised her hands so that her bracelets fell jangling down her arms. 'Then you don't win. At least you'll have tried.'

I suspected that Elise was just pretending that she wouldn't mind. There are people who are so used to winning, so used to being lucky, that they can't imagine it not happening.

* * *

The next morning we took my strip down to submit it. The entries went into a large box in the hotel foyer. As we put mine in, Eric came up with a large piece of paper rolled up with an elastic band round it.

'Hey, guys, good luck.' He tossed his roll of paper into the box casually as if it didn't really matter. Maybe it didn't, to him. Or maybe it was so good he didn't *have* to worry.

* * *

I found it really difficult to concentrate for the rest of the morning. I was sitting next to Eric in the 'Cartoon Styles' session and we were supposed to be drawing panels in the styles of different cartoonists, but I kept drawing Mum and Dad instead.

'Nice sketches. Who are they then?' Eric nodded at my notebook.

I panicked. 'No one.'

'Well, nice sketches of no one, Anzo,' Eric said, smiling. 'You're really good.'

'Thanks.'

'You don't sound too happy about it.' Eric had big round glasses that made his face look a bit like a wise owl. A wise owl with mad curly hair. For some reason I got the feeling I could trust him.

'You know when you really want something to happen, but then, when it does, it doesn't make you as happy as you thought it would?'

'Ah, yeah, I know that feeling, my friend.' Eric nodded, his glasses slipping down his nose (which made him look even wiser). He pushed back his chair a little bit and lowered his voice. 'There was this girl once. I had it so bad for her! You know what I'm talking about?'

I nodded as if I did and fiddled with my pen.

'I chased her for weeks – for months! And finally, *finally*, I got her to agree to go out to dinner with me. Anzo, when a woman you've wanted to notice you agrees to spend time with you, then that is a precious thing, yes?'

I nodded again. I understood the general feeling and thought that would probably do.

'So I thought really hard about where I would take her. It had to be special, it had to be perfect.'

It was obvious that Eric was enjoying telling this story. He was leaning back now, gesturing with his hand as if he was holding a pen and the story was a piece of paper in front of him. He reminded me of Dad.

'I read a hundred restaurant reviews! I studied

menus as if the secret to the evening going well was in the ingredients of every dish. I must have rehearsed every part of that night a thousand times. I really thought that it might be the first night of forever, you know?'

He pushed his glasses back up his nose and shook his head, as if he was remembering exactly how he felt.

'So what happened?'

'We got to the restaurant I'd picked out. I'd brought flowers. We were all dressed up. She looked amazing. She was everything I'd thought she would be. We sat down. We ordered some wine. We started talking. We'd only ever talked about general things before – you know, politics, music, that kind of thing.' Eric paused and broke into a huge grin. 'And then she asked what I liked to do most, what was my passion – and so I told her – I draw cartoons.'

'And?'

'And she said, "But cartoons are for kids."'

We stared at each other. 'But . . .' I didn't know where to begin.

'I know, I know, the love of my life and she didn't like cartoons!' Eric shook his head as if he still couldn't believe it.

I looked down at my sketches of Mum and

Dad. Is that how they felt about me? Maybe all the things I'd turned out to be weren't what they'd wanted, what they'd expected.

'Hey, don't look so sad, Anzo. It was all OK in the end,' Eric said.

'It was?'

'Sure.' Eric shrugged, putting out his arms with a wide-open gesture, just like Dad did. 'I just showed her my cartoons.'

'What happened?'

He grinned. 'She fell in love, Anzo, she fell in love.'

'With you or the cartoons?'

'Both!' he shouted.

We laughed and I felt a bubble of hope swell up in my chest.

* * *

My room and Elise's were right next to each other. We'd worked out a knocking code so that we didn't have to leave our rooms to communicate with each other. (We could have just used the internal phones, but that didn't seem as much fun.) Late that night I rapped out three knocks on the wall, our code for 'Are you awake?' but there was no answer.

I couldn't sleep. I kept thinking about the competition and whether I really minded about winning. A few weeks ago, winning something like that would have felt almost as important as growing taller. But now I was tall and things hadn't changed in the way I'd thought they would. It was starting to feel like getting what you wanted didn't always mean getting what you needed. And what I needed was the secret to making school and family life work. Could any competition do that?

I kept thinking about Mum and Dad. I thought about the way Dad sang 'Oh, What a Beautiful Mornin'' when he brought Mum her tea, and the way Mum thought the best time of day to hammer nails was half past eight in the morning because she reckoned it was a noisy time of day anyway. I thought about how Uncle Miles sometimes popped over first thing because he'd baked a batch of bread and liked us to have it fresh, while it was still warm, and how funny Uncle Talbert looked when he did an Irish jig.

Maybe they weren't missing me, but that didn't stop me from missing them.

To distract myself I downloaded Night Owl Bob's latest show to listen to before breakfast. The theme for the show was people who had escaped. I don't mean from prison or anything like that, but from jobs or awkward social situations or favours they'd been asked to do. Before Bob got people to call in he talked about this book where a boy pretended to really love the job he'd been given of painting a fence. His friends tried to make fun of him, but he ignored them as if he was so taken up with the painting that he couldn't drag himself away. All his friends were so convinced by his act they started giving him things in return for letting them have a go. The boy ended up not having to paint any of it. Night Owl Bob called it reverse psychology. Whatever it was, it made me wish I was as clever as that boy in the book. Maybe then I could make Josh think my size was OK, that I wasn't worth sniggering over every day. Maybe then I could find a way to be the right-shaped piece to fit the puzzle of my family.

It was funny how some people had gone to so much trouble to get out of something that wasn't that big a deal in the first place. For instance, there was a man called Stefan who'd been asked to pick up a parcel for his mum, but it meant he'd have to get up early on Saturday morning and he didn't want to miss his lie-in. So he told his mum that he couldn't do it because he had to get up really early to leave for a conference and do a presentation that he'd been specially selected to do. He figured that he might as well get a whole weekend of being undisturbed out of it since she was always ringing him up. But his mum felt so bad about him having to get up early that she came round first thing to make his breakfast. He ended up having to not only get up early but, just to keep up the pretence, he had to pack a bag and leave his own house to go to his made-up conference.

Maybe I wasn't trying to escape responsibility, but something about Stefan's story made me think of me and Elise. We'd travelled two hundred and fifty miles to make me feel happier, and it had worked, for now – but all my problems were still waiting for me at home.

Questions and Answers

The first thing I noticed about Jesse Edward was that he looked worried. His right leg was jiggling up and down as he sat watching us all file in and take our seats and he was drumming on his knees with his fingers. Maybe he didn't even realise he was doing it. I was a bit surprised – he was such a successful cartoonist that I didn't understand why he'd feel nervous – but when I mentioned it to Elise she tilted her head and looked at me oddly.

'*Everyone* gets nervous, Anzo. It's called being human.'

* * *

Jesse Edward had a deep, grumbly voice and smiled out of one side of his mouth. Everything he said surprised me. For instance, when someone asked him why he'd started drawing comics, he smiled. 'That's an easy question,' he said. 'I spent most of my childhood on my own. I wasn't very popular and so I withdrew into myself. And I suppose cartoons were the way I drew myself out – no pun intended!'

Everyone around me laughed, but I stared, wanting to make sure I didn't miss a word.

'Did being in the comic world help you then?' someone asked. 'I mean, help you to be happy?'

'Definitely. I mean, when I was a kid the thought of doing something like this, talking in front of a crowd –' he pretended to shudder and got another laugh – 'well, let's say I wasn't the world's most natural public speaker. I'm still not either!' (Another laugh.) 'But I think it all got better for me about a year after I got my first professional commission. It was basically a comic strip about being miserable in school – something I was kind of an expert in. And someone wrote me a letter to thank me. They said that a story I'd drawn had made them feel they weren't alone, that someone else knew what it was like. And it sounds crazy, but that's when I realised that *I* wasn't alone. Those words — someone else knowing what it's like — that made it all worth it.' He gave another lopsided smile. 'And I've been basically perfectly happy ever since.'

This time when everyone laughed, I joined in.

* * *

After the Q&A session, Elise started acting oddly. She kept looking around her and I had to repeat everything I said twice before she'd respond. All through the session on 'Cats in Cartoons' she was fiddling with her phone or glancing at the door. At the break I asked her what was going on.

'I don't know what you're talking about.'

'You're acting like you're wanted by the police or something.'

'No, I'm not.'

'Yeah, you are.'

'I'm just nervous about the competition, that's all.' Elise pushed her bracelets up her wrists and let them fall again.

I didn't believe her, but there's not much you can do if someone doesn't want to tell you something. Especially if that someone is Elise.

You Lose Some

The presentation for the competition was scheduled for two o'clock, right after lunch. There was going to be a brief summing-up of the whole convention by the organisers and thank-you's to everyone who had run the sessions, or generally helped out, and then they'd announce the results. That was what the woman who'd looked at me as if I was the wrong order of pizza told me and Elise. It turned out her name was Dee, and she was really nice now that she'd got over me not being the person she'd thought I was.

She even laughed about it a bit. 'You young lads say yes to everything — even when you don't have a clue what you're doing, don't you?'

'Yes,' I said, which made her laugh again.

Elise barely let me eat my sandwich before she was dragging me to the hall to get a seat at the front. 'Come on – we want to get a good spot.'

We found two places right up at the front, to the right of the gangway that went through the rows of seats. Elise looked back over her shoulder, as if she was checking the line of sight from our places to the big double doors. Then she nodded. 'Perfect.'

'What is?'

'Nothing.'

Which was typical really.

*　*　*

Dee was wrong about one thing. The summing-up wasn't brief. It went on for so long that my sleepless night caught up with me and I felt my head nodding forward. Elise had to nudge me hard in the ribs so that I didn't fall asleep. After the chief organiser, whose name was Mr Gilbert, had thanked everyone, from the session leaders to the caterers, he did a talk about the founders of the convention and the importance of cartoon strips to our daily lives. His talk lasted for about seventy-five years. Finally he finished up.

Everyone started sitting up straighter in their seats, shuffling their feet, readying themselves for the only part anyone was interested in now – the results of the competition. The convention would finish after the presentation, so everyone would be getting into their cars and onto buses and trains to get home. I suddenly had the urge just to get up and leave so that we could catch an earlier train. I wondered what Uncle Miles was cooking for dinner that night. I wondered if Mum had finished painting and whether the restaurant tables and chairs they'd ordered had arrived. I wondered if they'd decided on a name for the restaurant yet. Suddenly all I wanted was to go home.

'And now,' Mr Gilbert said, 'we have come to the moment I'm sure most of you have been waiting for – the announcement of the prize for the Best Cartoon of Comic Con.' He took a deep, dramatic breath. 'I have great pleasure in welcoming to the stage our first prize winner. The judges agreed that this was a superior piece of cartoon work demonstrating impressive technique and execution. Please come to the stage – Eric Durand!'

As the hall erupted with applause and Eric – beaming – made his way up to the stage, I turned to Elise and saw that she looked stricken. 'I'm so sorry, Anzo.'

'It's fine,' I told her. 'I didn't think I'd win.'

'But I thought you would!' Elise said.

I could have told her not to be so confident. The thing was, I was really OK with not winning. It wasn't just because I liked Eric; it was because it was good enough being here, with people like me, feeling part of it. Maybe the trophy would have helped things with my family, but maybe it wouldn't have. Being at the Comic Con had showed me that there were other people like me in the world, people who loved the same things I did, and that meant I wasn't really ever alone, even when I felt like it.

Elise wasn't taking my non-win so well though. And she still kept glancing behind us at the door.

Everyone kept on applauding as Mr Gilbert handed Eric the trophy. I put my fingers in my mouth and gave him a piercing whistle (something Dad taught me to do). He looked over at me and waved, giving me a thumbs up.

So I really was OK, and then I glanced behind me.

I stopped breathing for a second. Mum, Dad, Uncle Miles and Uncle Talbert were at the door.

I swivelled round to look at Elise.

'I'm so sorry,' Elise said again. 'I thought you'd win. I told them to come. I wanted them to see you, to show them how talented you are.' Her face had an 'I'm Really Sorry' look on it (something I wasn't used to seeing on Elise's face) and she was so still that even her bracelets were silent. 'I wanted to make you happy!'

I suddenly didn't feel quite so good about not winning. Not winning without my family watching was one thing; not winning with them watching was something else completely. It was just proving to them once and for all that I wasn't extraordinary.

'Anzo?'

'It's fine.'

But it wasn't.

And You Win Some

Eric walked off the stage and I kept glancing
back as my family slowly walked up the
gangway, blinking in the lights. 'Now, if
you'll all keep your seats for one more moment,
we have an unscheduled addition to the
programme.' I turned forward again to see Mr
Gilbert waving to signal that he hadn't finished.

'Although the judges selected a main
prizewinner, they were also unanimous in singling
out one other particular cartoon strip from the
hundreds of entries. They felt that this cartoon
was deserving of recognition for its emotional
honesty and fresh, unfettered, simple style.'

Elise reached out and clutched my arm. I was
conscious of my heart beating in my chest, like
it was echoing somehow.

I caught the eye of Dee, who was standing near Mr Gilbert. She grinned at me and winked. My face went hot, and then cold.

Mr Gilbert held up a piece of paper. 'Would Anzo Oliver come up and collect our brand-new Development Award for Outstanding Promise in Cartooning?'

For a second I felt like I'd forgotten how to breathe. I looked at Elise – she was grinning as if everything was finally as she'd expected it to be. She pushed me. 'Go on then.'

I stood up, still stunned. A wave of sound rose up in the hall – the sound of clapping.

'I told you you'd win,' Elise shouted over the noise. (Elise was right again so all was good with the world.)

I started to make my way up to the stage, my legs shaking.

'THAT'S OUR BOY!' Uncle Miles suddenly yelled out.

Mum, Dad, Uncle Miles and Uncle Talbert were almost at the top of the gangway now. I couldn't tell at first what their expressions were because of the angle of the lights. But what they were saying (yelling) kind of gave their feelings away.

'WOOOOHOOOO!' Uncle Talbert shouted.

A few people laughed, but in a nice way.

'GO GET YOUR HANDS ON THAT TROPHY, SON!' Dad shouted. And then everyone *really* laughed.

Especially when Mr Gilbert handed me the certificate instead of a trophy.

'Sorry about that,' he said apologetically. 'But you see, it's a new award so we actually only had the one trophy.'

'Oh, I don't mind,' I said. 'I don't mind at all. This is *great*.'

And it was.

*   *   *

Mum, Dad, Uncle Miles and Uncle Talbert surrounded me as soon as I got off the stage.

'Well done, Anzo,' Uncle Talbert boomed as he slapped me on the back.

'Fantastic work.' Uncle Miles gave me a bear hug that nearly suffocated me.

Mum took my certificate, beaming. 'I'll have to make a special frame to put this in, won't I?'

'You'll have to make two! Maybe three! This is just the start, isn't it, Anzo?' Dad slapped me on the back too. (I was quite keen for all the back-slapping to come to an end.)

I was a bit in shock. My family were here and they were all talking to *me*, not each other.

Some dreams don't come true like you expect them to. Sometimes it's even better.

Explanations

We still had to have a 'little chat' of course. I guess even Elise knew the whole lying-and-travelling-two-hundred-and-fifty-miles-on-our-own thing would have to be discussed. And after our apologies, it was time for explanations.

My mum and dad and uncles are the loudest, most *definite* people I know, but for once when I talked, they listened.

'Why didn't you *tell* us about how important cartoons are to you?' Mum said on the train. 'Did you really not think we cared about what you're interested in?' She pulled nervously at the ends of her scarf. It was covered in a pattern of little drills and planks of wood.

'I did try,' I said. 'Remember when I showed

you the Honourable Mention letter? I thought you weren't interested.'

Mum put her hand to her mouth. 'That? I thought it was something your school had made you do. And you looked so serious that I thought you were disappointed, not happy! I assumed you were hoping for a bigger prize so I was trying not to make a big thing about it.'

'It was a *great* result!' Elise told her.

Mum nodded and shifted in her seat. 'I get that now. I messed up.'

'But before this Honourable Mention that *we uncles knew nothing about*,' Uncle Talbert said, 'why didn't you tell us you draw these wonderful, amazing cartoons?'

Ever since we'd left the hotel, Mum, Dad, Uncle Talbert and Uncle Miles had been reading *Giant*.

'I guess because . . . they didn't feel amazing enough,' I said. 'You're all so confident and good at everything—'

'Hardly everything,' Uncle Talbert said. 'Think of Uncle Miles's sausages.'

'Oi!' Uncle Miles said. 'This from a man who wouldn't know filo pastry if he was *baked* in it.'

'Put a sock in it,' Dad told them.

And amazingly, they did.

'Go on, Anzo,' Mum said.

'I never felt good enough,' I said in a rush.

There was a silence. Probably the longest silence I've ever heard my family manage.

'Oh, *Anzo*,' Mum said. Her eyes were shiny. 'I'm so sorry.'

'The thing is, Anzo,' Dad said, 'your uncles and I grew up in a household that was very . . . difficult. Tradition, following the rules, doing what you were told was everything. With punishment when you didn't.'

'We were never encouraged to be ourselves,' Uncle Talbert agreed.

'We were never allowed to take risks, or to be loud, or to have any freedom,' Uncle Miles said. 'We were pushed towards things we didn't want to do, decisions we didn't want to make.'

'Your mother's parents were very protective too,' Dad went on.

Mum nodded. 'They meant well, but they wouldn't let me do anything on my own. Ever.'

'So when we had you, we wanted you to have the freedom to be who you are. Not to be steered towards things you weren't interested in. We were determined to give you the space to be your own person and not feel that we were telling you what to do and who to be.'

Dad sighed. 'But I guess in trying not to go in one direction, maybe we went too far in the other.'

'Yes,' Mum said. 'We got it completely wrong.'

Dad looked up and grinned, putting his hand on my shoulder. 'Well, maybe not completely wrong. Because look at you – you're wonderful!'

'Extraordinary,' Uncle Talbert said.

'For once I agree with you,' Uncle Miles said.

Mum squeezed my hand again. 'We'll try harder not to be so . . .'

'Over the top,' finished Dad.

'Over the top? *Us?*' Uncle Talbert stood up to demonstrate his outrage and hit his head on the luggage rack.

Uncle Miles yanked at his arm. 'Sit down, you idiot.'

Uncle Talbert sat down, with a big dramatic sniff. Uncle Miles rolled his eyes at me and I laughed. Dad was right – they were over the top. But they were mine. I leaned back in my seat smiling. We were still a hundred miles away from where we lived, but I already felt like I'd made it home.

But help is on the way . . .

NOT FOR LONG, SLIMY!

The net has turned.

Giant is strong . . .

And now Giant has friends . . .

AAAARRGH!

It's time for him to join them!

How Things Change

It's funny how you can want a big change to happen so desperately that you can hardly think about anything else. Then, when it happens, it happens in such a slow day-by-day way that you don't even realise it's happening at all. When we got back from the convention, it wasn't as if my family were suddenly talking to me all the time, or noticing everything I did, but little by little I started to feel that I belonged — that I had a part in our family play. For a start, Uncle Miles announced that I was going to be helping him in the kitchen.

'It's a scandal for a boy your age not to be able to make a cheese sauce,' he told me.

So Uncle Miles taught me how to make a

cheese sauce – and then how to make omelettes and risotto and Yorkshire pudding (the trick is really, really hot oil).

Then Mum decided that actually I should know how to change the washers on a sink. And once I knew that, she thought I might as well help her finish decorating the walls in the new toilets (the trick is to never buy cheap paintbrushes because you just end up forever picking loose hairs off the walls).

Best of all, Dad and Uncle Talbert told me they wanted me to do a daily cartoon on the specials board when the restaurant opened. 'Anything you like,' Dad said. 'You're the artist.' He didn't even say it as a joke.

Bit by bit I was doing stuff with my family, for my family. I even got up the confidence to tell them about Miss Bentley and her attempts to teach me seven different accents. It turns out that doing accents badly is just as funny as doing them well. I made them all laugh!

After the Comic Con, Eric and I started sending each other cartoons and he insisted on me joining his online cartoon critique group. He thought it was hilarious when he found out my age (I'd promised my family I'd come clean) and he immediately started to call me 'The

Prodigy'. It was the first nickname I'd ever had that I actually liked.

I was finally finding out what it felt like to be in a group. (It felt really good.)

I found a way to thank Elise too. Because without her, nothing would have changed. I knew now that sometimes you need a friend to nudge you in the right direction. (Or in Elise's case – shove.) And I wanted her to know that I appreciated her believing in my ability to be a winner, even when I didn't win in the way she expected. After giving it a lot of thought, Mum helped me find somewhere that sold specialist stationery and I bought an extra-large Post-it notepad divided into different colours. On the very top Post-it (purple) I drew Elise holding up a book called *The Secret to Happiness*. Under that I wrote: 'For Elise, a big friend at any height.'

When she read it she was quiet for about five minutes, which has to be a record. Then she hugged me so hard I couldn't breathe and about six seconds after that she was bossing me around again and everything was back to normal. Except it was all much, much better. She framed my drawing and hung it on her wall but apparently if I ever get famous, she's going to sell it to the highest bidder. (She probably would, too.)

* * *

School changed as well. The week after the Comic Con, Miss Bentley decided that Josh would make a great evil stepmother in *Snow White and the Seven Dwarfs*. I didn't really feel the need for any revenge after that – real or fantasy. Then somehow (thanks, Elise), everyone at All Stars Primary found out that I had impersonated a grown-up and won an award. The day after that went round, I walked into my class and Nathan said, 'All right?' and after that, well, I was. So these days when I walk in, that's what I get – 'All right?'

In the end, for me, that's what happiness is. It's being all right.

* * *

Oh, and in case you were wondering, when the restaurant opened its name was . . .

'Anzo's'.

Acknowledgements

This book is dedicated to Sara Grant, who has been responsible for kick-starting so many writing careers in children's publishing – including mine. Sara is an enormously talented author; an exceptional communicator and connector of people; and a warm, witty, generous and loyal friend.

A book is always a team effort, but sometimes one person is more responsible for the result of the published pages than any other. Tilda Johnson, the editor for *Giant*, must take the majority of credit (or guilt) for this book's existence. She encouraged me to submit ideas, selected *Giant* as being the most promising, and then steered me as I navigated my way around the inevitable narrative potholes with admirable (and apparently endless) patience and humour. I am so grateful for her insightful, thoughtful edits and warm encouragement. Editors don't always get a big enough thank you – so Tilda, please accept my GIANT thanks here. (Yes, I know.) I also need to thank Felicity Johnston, who took over the editorial reins when Tilda left to pursue an adventure of her own. Fliss made the editorial transition feel utterly smooth and seamless and was so giving of her energy and enthusiasm that it felt as if she'd been cheering the book on from the very beginning. Huge thanks too to my fantastically efficient agent Eve White, Talya Baker, the sharp-eyed and meticulous copy editor, and the rest of the supportive and fantastic Piccadilly team: marketing manager Charlotte Hoare, PR manager Tina Mories and proofreader Ilona Jasiewicz.

More outsized thanks are due to nicandlou, responsible for the absolutely brilliant cover and artwork and giving the book exactly the right visual feel.

And finally, colossal thanks are due to my family, for their daily love, support and encouragement. There isn't a tape measure in the world that could calculate the extent of my love for them.

Kate Scott

The first book in Kate Scott's comedy-adventure series for Piccadilly, *Spies in Disguise: Boy in Tights*, won a Lancashire Fantastic Book Award, and books in the series have been published in Denmark and the USA. Kate has written fiction and non-fiction for Oxford University Press, Pearson, HarperCollins and Hodder. She is also a published poet, a playwright and a scriptwriter for children's television.

Thank you for choosing a Piccadilly Press book.

If you would like to know more about our authors, our books or if you'd just like to know what we're up to, you can find us online.

www.piccadillypress.co.uk

You can also find us on:

We hope to see you soon!